THE

Fairlane

INCIDENTS

The FAIRLANE Series

THE
Fairlane
INCIDENTS

NICK SAVAGE

4 Horsemen
Publications, Inc.

4 Horsemen
Publications, Inc.

4 Horsemen Publications, Inc.
1497 Main St. Suite 169
Dunedin, FL 34698
4horsemenpublications.com
info@4horsemenpublications.com

Cover by S. Casagrande
Typesetting by Valerie Willis
Editor 4 Horsemen Publications, Inc.

Library of Congress Control Number: 2022932807

Paperback ISBN-13: 978-1-64450-551-9
Audiobook ISBN-13: 978-1-64450-549-6
Ebook ISBN-13: 978-1-64450-550-2

DEDICATION

For Kris, my love and my inspiration.

Table of Contents

CHAPTER I

Wonder What's Next

I stand outside a greasy hamburger stand, shaking my head of purposefully unkempt hair in both awe and amused disappointment of the greater City Beautiful that surrounds me. Yet, there is an enchanting magic in this warm Orlando summer night as the mix of tourists and locals, all dressed in a variety of T-shirts, cargo shorts, and flip-flops or sandals, wander about. I look past them toward the giant buildings with facades designed like a drunk developer binged on the Mouse and his movies too much the night before, finished the night off with *Vegas Vacation*, and then made his distorted, haunting dreams into one long, wonderfully tacky street known as West Irlo Bronson Memorial Drive. I stand, shaking my head because I know it is here I am meant to be. Here is where I will find my inspiration.

I notice a man staring at me through a crowd of mismatched tourists. An ordinary enough looking man in his mid to late twenties. He's a bit bewildered. I look at him and nod. He thinks he knows me. Recognizes me from somewhere but can't place where. I've seen this look before... many times. It's fun watching the wheels turn in their heads as they try figuring out if I'm a friend, foe, ex-lover, or something else. I don't want to stare too long; you never do. It gets weird for them long before it gets weird for me. His face lights up. He tries to keep it subtle, but I see. He's figured out why I look familiar. His first encounter with a star—fading or otherwise. He realizes I'm Finn Fairlane, producer and songwriter extraordinaire, muse to the stars. He nods, smiles, and says he loves my work. I am far enough away that I didn't actually hear him say those words (not that it matters to him) but I've learned to read lips a bit over the years. If only a few phrases.

He walks off as I wait for my food outside this borderline edible, walk-up hamburger joint, taking in all of Kissimmee/Orlando's once glorious tourist trap Old Town, as the conversations of others continue to drone in the background like multiracial noise. The screams from teen girls as the Vomatron whips them around and around at seventy-five miles an hour dot the verbal cacophony like an overdriven crash cymbal in a Nine Inch Nails song. Ah!... Ah!... Ah!... But my attention slowly shifts, and the noise builds and swells like "Pinion," overtaking my visual attention. Just when it all amplifies, layering sound upon sound upon sound, so much my ears cannot stand the noise anymore, it falls away like the end of "Hurt."

It all stops.

For all I know, I could have gone deaf. The world around me could have caught fire. Hell, I could have been on fire. But none of that would have registered on my radar this second. Gleaming under the glow of the streetlamps and neon stars is beautiful, porcelain (just sweaty enough on this hot, summer night to be sexy) cleavage. I can't notice anything else. I am stuck in this moment, my eyes are feasting, and mouth-watering fantasies start to form. I am a man, after all; of course my eyes are drawn to her (what I'm guessing is a full C) cleavage. Also, to the elaborate ink on her left arm peeking out from her rolled-up sleeve: the beautiful color palette of black, blues, reds, greens, gold, and more making what, at first glance, seems to be a collage of superheroes. A woman after every man's heart.

As I was saying, there's something magical in these warm, summer, Orlando nights. A magic that makes the already large droves of people grow even more massive as the sun goes down. The gentle breeze that cools off the warmth of the day. The sky-line of countless billboards, resort hotels, discount gift shops, restaurants, and churches to the gods of gaud-iness and gluttony from the day that plunges into the vast, stark night. A deep purple night sky, polka-dotted with neon constellations of Vomatrons, Slingshots, sky coasters, and anything else advertisers can backlight to bleed tourists' pockets dry. Despite all that, this is where I belong. This city quietly calls to my fast-ap-proaching, middle-aged self, making similar, sweet promises whispered by Hollywood to young star-lets. To inspire. To be my muse. I know it. I feel it in my bones—a fast, agitating force that overcomes my senses, my muscles, my body. A feeling of being inspired that only comes along once in a great while. I feel it here.

What different musings I may find here compared to my time in New York or Chicago, I do not know. I left behind what life I had made for myself in the Big Apple: the chart-topping clients I produced in the music industry; my three-bedroom, three-bath brownstone; the few people I would call friends. I followed an internal calling, or an external beckoning if you will, to travel south. I'm not sure if it's an idiosyncrasy solely reserved for artists, the small, nagging child called wanderlust nudging me along, or maybe my deep-seated need to uproot my life once I start to find a comfort zone. I heard it calling me over and over again. It had been calling to me for a while, and Finn Fairlane listens to the call. Yes, I do. I apparently also refer to myself in the third person sometimes. But moving on.

The taxi top ads, radio, and television commercials all advertising Florida vacations. The dead-inside feeling that comes with working for big-name labels. Writing songs that had no passion left in them, only the ability to make dollar signs. I wanted something more. The internalized, unstoppable, ongoing struggle to better this thing I have come to call myself. Always moving, pushing forward. And it whispered over and over to me, "Orlando." To this, I listened. I am here.

It is my first night living in the endless summer that is Orlando, the city next door to that magical kingdom. That beautiful machine of childhood joy and adult misanthropy and cynicism. Dreamt up to make you forget the prejudice, arrogance, and misogyny with which it was built. Designed so each step farther inside makes you believe in your childhood more and more, washing away the jaded eyes of adulthood.

But that is Orlando.

Look past the epidemic of crystal meth, coke, and heroin so evident on these Florida streets in the leather-skinned, emaciated man with long, wispy hair as he twitches uncontrollably in his dirty, torn rags, or in the missing teeth of the haggard woman as she begs for change. Not just in Old Town, or Kissimmee, or even Orlando, but the whole of Florida. Look past it all because there you will find a place where the original concept 4,022 miles west could be so abominated by corporate culture to create something so wonderfully tacky, invitingly dominating, monstrously huge, and still pale in comparison to the egos of the people who run the place. Maybe, it's just what I see.

Welcome to Orlando.

And the city welcomes me with her. This fair-skinned beauty. Inked in all the right places and a look in her eye of deviant desires. She notices me leering. Since I'm standing not too far from where she waits in line and leering is meant to be obvious, I shouldn't be surprised she saw me, but I am. Not so much that she caught me, but that she didn't look away. Is this how fans feel when they recognize me? The roles have reversed because I am a fan of hers. I try to hold my surprise inside. I try not to react, but something gives it away. Perhaps an involuntary upturn of the corner lip. Or an unknowing eyebrow raise. Something gave my surprise away because she smiles, just a little.

Just enough to let me know she knows, and that she's okay with it.

Her hazel eyes, outlined in the blackest of black liner that extends just past her corners, stay connected with mine. Ready to devour. A fleck in her left eye, accented by an eyebrow ring, adds to the allure. What some would deem an imperfection only makes this stare sexier. There's something about her stare. Hauntingly familiar, like a scene from my memory playing out in front of my eyes. We keep each other's gaze. A slow waltz of our eyes in our minds. A waltz that gently takes her closer to me, dancing around the unspoken subject of the moment. Who speaks first? I'm dancing with this stranger. Neither of us whispers a word. Just dancing and waiting. Observing her as she watches me.

This dance is pleasant. Like the joy of the earlier drive down I-4 to my new abode. Waltzing through clear traffic. I was taking in my new surroundings at 80 plus miles an hour. Screaming along in my 80-grit voice to post-Black Flag, Rollins Band's song (though some could argue I was blaring Mother Superior) "I Want So Much More," popping my speakers while passing palm tree after palm tree. Broken and abandoned cars scattered along the median and shoulders, momentary scabs on the city's beauty. As my pepper hair that has become dashed with salt blows in the wind of the open windows, I looked at the intertwining highways that make up the circulatory system of this city; I couldn't help wondering how my life would get intertwined into this city's lifeblood. I have yet to find where I fit into this metropolis among the more than two million people that run around this semi-tropical paradise every day. I will discover my place, though.

I do take note of the irony of the green dominating the floral pattern on her low-cut, button-down blouse. The green flora lines her bosom like the palms line the highway. Her shirt says to me, "Come, drive here." Take that for what you will. For a split moment, though, I ask myself why I know it's a low-cut, button-down blouse. Then I see the gentle bite she gives her bottom lip that gently pushes out her snake bite studs, and my manhood returns to me. That simple gesture says it all. Green she is anything but, and I want to know how far from green she is. I have to play it cool. React too strongly and come off as the upturned collar, golfer cap, polyester-wearing, wild and crazy guy. Play it too cool, and she'll think we both play for the same team. So, I do the only thing my muscles will allow me to do, as my mind unhooks her bra to reveal breasts that could bring a nation to its knees. With every ounce of my being, I summon the primordial gods of love and lust to give me power. They look down and bestow upon me the almighty ability to smile and give a slight nod.

I fucking smile and give a slight nod.

I've flirted before, hundreds of times, thousands even. This evening is no different from any of my previous one-night stands, three-night stands, or the plethora of quasi-relationships I've had. They all begin the same way: a subtle look, a dog-eat-dog-sly smile, a wink. God forbid a word, like hello. Something small. Though tonight, all my wiles abandon me in my moment of need. So, I smile and nod. Play it cool though. Wait for her to come to me.

Or am I wrong? Is this just a chick oiling her engine for a steamy night with her man? Damn. Am I the pregame mental porn she's using to rev her freshly oiled engine? Some real-life, soft-core PornHamster clip playing out in her mind to fantasize about later? (Which is a fantasy in and of itself for me.) Am I being used in her mental game?

Perchance this could be my first intertwining with the city. Perchance to sin. With her.

Perchance.

Then again, it was for this "perchance" that I left my life in New York behind me. Finished up album productions, cover concepts, and whatever other current affairs I had with clients and said, "Adios." Bid my fond adieus to the giant, light-polluting, prostitute-ridden, yet ever endearing and always loved area known as Times Square. Said goodbye to my favorite bartender at Sunswick 35/35 in Astoria. Stood there for one last moment, my hazel eyes taking it all in. The cool, crisp air slightly stung my weather-worn face on a chilly night, adding to my growing crow's feet as I squinted through the cold. Not sure when, or if, I'd ever breathe in New York air again. A part of me wanted to stay. A part of me wanted never to leave that moment because that moment was the accumulation of everything I've done in my life.

It was hard to believe it could ever be better than it ever was. But it was calling me—the stranger in the night that was Orlando. I was unsure if Orlando would be what I expected, except that I had no expectations.

A part of me knew that it would be okay. That it would be the right place to be. But I stood there, engraving that moment in my mind: the green and brown leaves on the trees, the cars that lined the street, brick building after brick building housing countless people I'd never know, the sounds of people laughing a block away, the sirens in the distance, and the wind blowing against me. The love I feel for that great city, all of it. I took a mental snapshot of that moment in time before I got into my car. I drove off into the sunset (well, sunset on my right since I was heading south). The poetry fits better, however, if I had driven into it.

Not every client was happy to see me go, and that's understandable. That's a good thing for me. It means I've done my job, but I can't help my clients if I have nothing that inspires me. I can't muse my people, produce records, write songs, and do what I do if I have no muse myself to inspire those things, to make me want to create something bigger than myself. New York is a city that has endless inspiration for some. CBGB launched the careers of many musicians and inspired countless more. New York is the city of Gershwin. Cole Porter. The city of Philip Roth and Woody Allen. Every turn hides something new. From a mouse scavenging for food to the beauty in the blue-gray eyes of a homeless man that still clings to hope, to the stories you hear from the old woman sitting in the corner seat at your local bar. The late-night coke deals at gas stations with NYPD's finest filling up a pump away, to the bartender betraying the location of all the security cams so you can smoke inside when it's ten below and windy outside. Screaming Andrew

W.K.'s "I Love New York City" at the top of your lungs when you're three sheets to the wind. Every day something new. Something wonderful.

But for me, I had somehow managed to over-stay my welcome in a city of over eight million. When everywhere you turn you see memories of a better time, you don't feel inspired. You don't feel much like writing lyrics. Don't feel much like turning up the snare or adjusting the EQ of the floor tom. You don't feel much like doing anything. I found myself wallowing in my studio, quickly becoming the brooding musician the nineties were so rife with. Even my hair is in that in-between stage of long and short, either in dire need of a haircut or a better way to style it. I hated those brooding musicians and hated myself for becoming something I hated. So, I left. I left before I got stuck in a routine that spiraled downward, unable to ever get up. I needed to see what the next place held for me. And it was Orlando that called.

The eye contact we held breaks, returning me from my thoughts about New York as the hamburger stand worker hands her an already melting vanilla cone she promptly lifts to her deep red lips. Red lip-stick that deep in color makes a statement that she takes control. She gets what she wants. I hope she wants me. A drop of melted ice cream disappears into her radiant, porcelain cleavage. Somehow that falling bit of ice cream makes me notice her long, curly, jet-black hair, unnoticed before perhaps because her hair disappears into the now black of the night sky above. Illuminated only by the surrounding neon stars. Maybe because her cleavage and eyes consume me in an all-encompassing fire that can only be doused by her. But now I notice. Curly hair is sexy. Almost dangerous. Curly haired ladies are the kind that breaks hearts. The kind of girl you don't bring home to your mother. Yes. Curly haired girls are super freaks.

It won't get to the point of heartbreaking. She will take control of nothing tonight, at least not with me. Or perhaps she already has and I just don't know it yet. Our moment seems to be over now that her creamy treat on a cone is delivered. She walks away from the pick-up window and past me as I stand, still waiting on my food to be made. She smiles as she passes and whispers something.

"Fate?"

"Feint?"

"Eighth?"

Hell. Did she say, "freight?" Did she want me to ship something? Is she looking for weed? A little Mary Jane for tonight? I couldn't hear clearly. The screaming man on the Slingshot and the laughter of his female companion drowns out the clarity of her word. She could have said, "Take me right here and now," and I would have been none the wiser. My mind is frantically going over every word, every phrase she could have said, and each time my mind thinks of something new that is more obtuse than the thought before. This deluge of thoughts makes my mind think more and get caught in a pattern that only makes things worse. A game of telephone I play with myself, ever distorting the original phrase spoken. All this because she enthralls me, and I'm unable to say something cool in hopes of releasing tension later on. But at least

I won't be the only one not getting any tail tonight. I'm sure whatever man card the guy on the Slingshot held was stripped away the moment he started screaming like a preteen girl at a J. Bieb concert.

Did I get her name? Was it a message? The name of a place, perhaps? Maybe the heartbreaking does start tonight. For that one fleeting moment, it hurts. A hurt I haven't felt since I lost a $10,000 hand of blackjack at Circus Circus in Reno. I may have been up that $10,000 and playing with the house's money, but for a few moments, my table was surrounded by people with all eyes on me and that moment was mine. Those ten-thousand dollars in one hand. Only a few seconds for the card to flip and the dealer to win. For those few moments, though. For those few moments, that money was mine.

And for a few, she was mine. For a fleeting moment, we were cosmically entangled. A planet-sized meteorite on a crash course for earth, ready to make extinct all previous carnal knowledge I possessed. But no, Bruce Willis and his ragtag team of oil rig drillers had to blow her up. Had to destroy what could have awakened in me some previously undiscovered Chakra. It's cool though, Bruce. You killed Hans Gruber.

I whip my head around to see if she is still looking at me. I could have been more discreet, but after the leering and the ever-so-smooth smile and nod, I figure, "Fuck it." So a whip of my head it is. But no. A man whose dated, gigantic, arm-wrapped tribal tattoos and overly sculpted muscles make him look as though he's preparing for gladiatorial, hand-to-hand combat in a real-life version of a Bethesda© Softworks game has his arm around her shoulder. His shoulder blades bulge out of his bleached white tank top. The style of tank top that is often associated with either domestic violence or under-educated people of Mediterranean descent. His carefully frayed, bootcut jeans sag off legs that have been bullied out of every day in the gym by his over-sized torso. He leans down, his lips entwining with hers.

How I wish those were my lips pressing against hers. They look so soft, like a moist red velvet cake. So ready to taste something new. My arm wrapped around her shoulder. Or waist.

I watch them, casually. Or at least what I think looks casual. Nonchalant. I want to know how she feels about him. To understand why she flirted with me. I want to know why the hell I'm so entranced with her. No conversation. No physical contact. Just one muddled and misunderstood word she whispered.

They continue walking after an all-too-short public display of dwindling affection. Dying love could mean good news for me. I think. If I'm right. If I ever see her again. She turns her head back to me and winks her flecked eye. Damn that eye, both eyes. Haunting. They disappear into his metallic blue '98 Camaro, flames painted on the hood and sides to give the illusion of going really fast. I always thought that's what the pedal on the right was for. Hell, I'd bet ten to one he only drives with two pedals.

So here I am, left standing, abandoned by my wiles and by fate. But I smile. Soaking in both my surroundings and the events of the evening: the modern-day, casino-free Reno, the not-so-redneck Pigeon

Forge, the little Vegas strip. This street numbered 192. At this moment in my life, I know this is where I need to be, where the winds of fate and fortune want to steer me. So, I stand outside the neon lilac and turquoise gate of Old Town, staring across the street at a shop I shorten to "Chine Gun 'Murica" with giant gift shops next to other giant gift shops. All of which brings "trying too hard" to whole new levels, with exterior murals painted top to bottom and oversized, eye-catching relief art. Not great art, mind you. Just eye-catching enough to put their vanilla overtones off.

Then you see the ad. "Gifts here. Towels at $3.99." But inside, they are all filled with the same gifts: generic clothes and countless items all stamped with that symbolic, mouse-eared "D" or ORLANDO sprawled across it. Items that end up collecting a half inch of dust on a shelf in a cabinet not long after purchase. But in these stores, they scream to be purchased. Puppies in a kennel crying out for a new home if you will. It's all so you can buy stuff as your reminder of time spent here, which I am all for. But if you are going to surround yourself with stuff, just make sure it's the right stuff.

Damn. Damn it all. I can only laugh at the events of the night.

What the hell did she say to me? And what did it mean? If I don't know what she said, I guess the meaning is pretty much a cow's opinion. Moo. Pointless. Yes, it's moot, I know, but I heard that somewhere once, probably on some hotel room tv while watching some sitcom rerun about a bunch of friends or something, and it stuck. So, moo it is. On the other hand, if I can figure out what she said, then I can ponder the meaning more.

Moo.

I am here surrounded by people, drifting in the loneliness of the passing moment. I wonder what's next. Tonight, the fates gave me a teaser of an intro to this city in the form of my mystery woman instead of a hands-on preview. Fine. I'm okay with that because as I'm standing here, inspiration swirls around me: from the clothes worn by the line of people waiting to eat a burger, to the cars that drive in and out of Old Town, past the Ferris wheel, to the distant early 2000's pop rock playing that barely carries this far. I find inspiration in everything around me.

In this moment, I take what I can—everything that it is this night. And a fantastic night it is. The sounds of young lust and fading innocence that gets so quickly pushed away. The never-been-kissed girl in braided pigtails flirting with the leather-clad rebel boy who is finally showing interest. He makes some joke I can't hear, but she laughs and playfully hits him. She makes her move and kisses him. A moment of unsure shock and joy on his face, but then he grabs her and pulls her in. They make a connection. The collision of two souls, intersecting on this path we call life, coming together in a moment of glorious happenstance. If only for a moment. She will never be the same. I can see her quiver with anticipation. His hands slowly slide down her back, stopping at her hips. She puts her hands on his as if to stop him, interlacing her fingers with his.

The girl hesitates, squeezing his hands for a moment. She lets that linger, enjoying the moment as their lips explore each other. She untangles her fingers and moves her hands, running her unsure fingers through his hair. He pulls her in closer, trying to have both bodies occupy the same space at the same time. Defy the laws of physics, good sir! If there's ever a time to defy them, it's now. It is this moment that begins the loss of her, or both of their, innocence. She'll spend as much time trying to lose it as she will regretting who she lost it to. But tonight, beneath the neon stars of the night sky, none of that matters. Just this moment is all that's important. The right here and right now. A fleeting moment we all try to hold on to as long as we can. Each time it happens, every time it happens.

Damn her eyes. I return to my forest green Grand Am. Two Door. Nice stock rims. Nothing that screams "I have a tiny penis!" but not understated. I blink as I open the door and her eyes haunt me. I can't remember the last time I saw eyes that were both so serene yet so filled with raw energy. Such potential energy waiting to explode in a nails-deep-in-my-flesh, sweat-dripping, soul-connecting, tangled-tongues-and-lips sex session that can only lead to both of us in the midnight hour crying, "More! More! More! More!" All I do is blink.

While this first night is not quite the start to my time here like I hoped, it sticks with me. Not just because it is my first night, but because of the events of the evening. The haunting familiarity of her gaze sticks in my mind, an icy reminder of what should have, or more properly stated, could have transpired tonight. It haunts me over the next eight weeks as

I unenthusiastically gather clients to try and inspire, produce, and make great. I say unenthusiastically not because I'm not happy to be getting new clients, but because I know as of right now, I can't properly do what I do.

Damn those eyes.

CHAPTER 2

She's Gone

I settle into my soundproof studio, reading the news on my phone of the approaching tropical storm and its growing momentum. The schoolyard bully that is my computer's screensaver teases me as it scrolls across the monitor. It yells, calling me on my procrastination, "Get Back To Work." As if I don't know that behind the black wall of words is a program waiting to record my lyrical genius. Waiting for me to create, to bring to life a new Finn Fairlane musical masterpiece for the world to embrace as its new anthem. The spontaneous birthing of new and exciting ideas is why I came here. To be inspired. To write. To create.

My deep purple, sometimes black depending on the way the light hits it, six-string Washburn sits strapped around my shoulder. Condenser microphone hides behind the pop screen in its stand, tempting me to say something. Anything. Some simple phrase sung into its steel mesh that brings it bursting to life.

Pen and notebook on a silver music stand next to me. Lyrics lying in wait to scribble themselves onto paper, but I sit empty-headed on my stool. Nothing. My mind feels constipated. Too much mental cheese stops up the tubes. When I try to play, it gives forth no sound. Its wires do not vibrate nor give music. I sit a music-less musician. Geddy Lee would be so disappointed in me right now.

I've had writer's block before: times when nothing good comes to mind, when the words I write are more representative of a junior high girl scribbling love notes about the cute boy across the room than lyrics written by an Emmy-winning professional, when the words read more like "Without You" than "Kickstart My Heart." Blocked times when music I write sounds more reminiscent of a bad video game soundtrack from the days of first-gen Game Boy and not so much the rock 'n roll it's supposed to be, stuff I should have tried selling to I Fight Dragons. Those gents could have made the riffs worthy, but I can't recall a time when nothing comes to mind, a time when all my creativity abandoned me—the unwanted dog left on the side of a central California county road.

Don't get me wrong; I've never done such an inhumane thing as leaving a dog. One afternoon, however, I was driving through (what some would call) a town east of Merced, California. The brown landscape of dead and dying plant life, underfed cows, sheep, and livestock surrounded me as far as the eye could see. The only savior to this was the occasional tree that had managed to somehow thrive in this Easy-Bake Oven the cartographers call the Central Valley. That and the rolling hills and mountains on the distant horizon to break the monotony. But there I was, driving through the isolation when a rundown, rust-coated, white-and-brown suburban a little way ahead of me coasted to a stop. The kind of stop that somehow seemed more like a skeezy leisure suit skulking his way to an unsuspecting female than a van coming to a stop.

As they did stop, they let out a dog. The suburban sped away. Nothing too fast, just accelerated as if the situation was typical. I kept driving, thinking nothing of it. Until later that night when I returned down the same road and the dog was still there, unmoved from where it first sat down all those hours ago. The good soldier he was, seated at attention, awaiting orders from his sergeant, little did he know his commanding officer was never to return. So, I called out to him. He remained unmoved.

I took some caution in my approach, knowing the worst that this thirsty mutt would try is a meager attempt at a defensive bite. But he sat resolutely. No collar. No name. Just a sad, short-haired mutt: white, brown, and covered in fleas. I'm sure the state of the dog reflected the conditions inside the vehicle. I petted him—soft and gentle. Tried to turn my 80-grit voice into something a little less rough. More 800-grit but the best I think I was able to muster was 120. He started to perk up. Tail wagging, tongue hanging out from dryness. I coaxed him my way and into my car. It didn't take me long to name him: Lieutenant Dan. It somehow seemed to suit.

Much like Lieutenant Dan when I found him, I sit abandoned. I refuse to be the one that's deserted. I leave my guitar and microphone. I am the white-and-brown truck, not the dog. For the moment, I leave them behind. Guitar and mic stand at attention—waiting for me, the obedient dogs they are. I'll be back. Just not right now.

I need to get my writing mojo back. I haven't had any since before moving down here, and it's not coming back. To paraphrase the immortal words of Maynard James Keenan, I need it, even though I don't want it. To breathe, feel, and know I am very much living. Without it, I feel useless, lifeless. A shell of a man attempting to live in a world in which he has already died. The ability to tap into an emotion that isn't readily there and write from it is what makes me Finn. To put myself in another's shoes and feel what they feel is something that comes to me—usually at the ready—but doesn't come at all for others. There is this innate ability to become someone else for a few moments: enough to write, to make music, to have an authentic feel as if I've lived those moments over and over again. I can't do any of those because my mojo is gone. New York pulled it all out of me. The few clients I've taken on in the two months I've been down here are more than grateful, but in all honesty, they are getting the short end of the Finn Fairlane stick. I don't give the short end in any situation. I give a huge, long, rock-hard stick. And it all comes from mojo. I'm still a stranger in a strange land. So, I do what anyone in need to see something inspiring would do: grab my car keys off the ledge by the door and drive.

It would seem the gods of rock 'n roll are not on my side today. Two miles onto I-4 and the traffic slows to a crawl. Who knows why it slowed down—stalled car, horrific wreck with blood all over the road, a slow-moving truck that's trying to change lanes, out-of-state driver. Could be anything. Though it gets me thinking about this machine that is Orlando. Built West Coast by one man. One wildly misogynistic man and a dream. And he did it. He built it all. His corporate team of money-hungry, bloodsucking, anything-for-a-dollar white collars continue to build on his dream. Perhaps bigger than he could have imagined. Maybe this larg-er-than-life monstrosity is how he precisely imagined it. Maybe that's the problem. I don't dream big enough anymore. Instead of just building a park, he built a park and a town. Bought land and built more. And more. And more. And more. And people came. I came. I've written songs. Sold songs to the best of them. But the well ran dry. It's why I'm here. No offense, Fred, but if Limp Bizkit can arise from this, I sure as shit can rise again.

I turn on the radio to rambling tropical storm updates. Tropical storm Castle Heat, Cataratan, or whatever it's named, has been officially upgraded to a category one hurricane, which sounds extremely dan-gerous, but this far inland, it's more wind and rain than actual destruction, if it ends up even making landfall. And with that long-winded yet otherwise seemingly mundane announcement, a ton of bricks from the late nineties blares out of the speakers, hitting me straight across the face. As a ton of bricks racking your face should do, it reminds you of something. Mostly some-thing you forgot. This song so eloquently refreshes my memory that it was all done for the nookie. If ever more juvenile, yet truer words were spoken. Only in Limp Bizkit's hometown of Orlando—well, Jacksonville, but to the geographically challenged and purposes of my locale, all Florida is just Orlando—can you still hear this song twenty years past its relevance without it being a call-in request. Ah, the good ole' days of pay for play. But true the words were. I don't know any prepubescent teens who pick up a guitar thinking, *It's all about the art, man.* No. They pick it up thinking sex, drugs, and rock 'n roll. It's what it's about.

Rock 'n roll is the embodiment of it all. Hot females dripping with baby oil, ready for action. Guys ready to give and receive. It's the musician's setting that encourages such great, uninhibited hedonism. Coke-fueled orgies that end in chain-smoking cigarettes and Mary Jane for an hour or two. And somehow this piece of shit song is reminding me of exactly what I need.

Nookie.

Damn you, Durst.

But damn him as I may, he was right. So, I do what every red-blooded American does while idling in bumper-to-bumper traffic. I swipe right on my blood red-and-black cased cellphone and make a call. The statistics show that driving on your cellphone is the same as driving drunk, but I, much like every other driver on the road, don't think that statistic applies to me, them. You know. Self-entitlement is the backbone of today's society. Especially in an area that outcries for the death of every alligator because of the unfortunate death of one small child. Unfortunate it was, but to place the life of one child above countless alligators in the lake to calm the masses is what makes Dismal

Land the pretty-hate machine that it is. Quelling innumerable lives behind the scenes, keeping it out of the public eye, just to keep the look of their park clean and the grand illusion maintained. It's moments like this I hope, deep in my soul, karma has something big in store for the damned rodent.

At least my client answers his phone.

"D.B. What's up, my man?!" I say, knowing damn well he's sitting in his studio either surfing *Imgur Gone Wild* for boob shots of exes or dickin' around on his eight-string guitar. The eight-string guitar. I have such mixed feelings about that thing. If you want to play an instrument that gives off such low tones, play bass. On the other hand, the damned thing does give them a sound that a six-string could not. So, I keep my opinions to myself. Mostly.

"Working on some new stuff. Down for a few?" he replies, already knowing my answer.

D.B., short for Danny Boyle, is a good guy. In my short months here, he and his bandmates are one of the few clients I like beyond the work and enjoy doing anything with. Possibly the only. D.B. has bright, fire-engine red hair that hasn't changed since his infancy. The only reason I know that is his mother stopped by the studio my first session with them to drop off some homemade beef-and-cabbage soup. What an underrated dish that is. The smell of it might be enough to put some people flat on their asses, but the smell aside, it's one of my top five favorite dishes after that day.

Eileen Boyle can cook. Also, one good-looking lady too. Long red hair. Waves that almost turn it curly.

Pale-blue eyes. Light freckles dotting her thin frame, concentrations around her high cheekbones. Eyes inset just deep enough to give her an almost perpetually sorrowful look. But her smile lights up the room.

After the first time I met her, there were these fantasies that started to creep into my mind. I didn't want them to creep in; they just would. Like a yearning for a cigarette each time you try to quit. I just thought of her in that flowing, blue & cream bohemian-chic dress she wore the day of the soup. They were choice fantasies too. Her hand slides up the inside of my shorts to tease me a bit. My hand works its way up her shirt to gently pull on her nipple. Some start in full session. Her legs wrap around me as I fill her up inside, embracing in hours-long passionate kisses. They were fantasies like that. Half-chubbed before getting anywhere juicy with them. I wouldn't let myself get anywhere juicy with them. I had to cut my mental movies short because every time I wanted to run with them, I knew two things. One, each time I started fantasizing about her, all I could think of is that scene from *The Goonies* where they find that large rock and Martha Plimpton says, "Brand, God put that rock there for a reason..." He moves it anyway, and bats fly out. Which brings me to two: Some things are best left unexplored.

It all started because I noticed her in a certain light. Literally. The light hit her in a way that made her look more aged, and she still looked beautiful. Perhaps, in a way, more than she is. She's always going to look graceful. She noticed me too. Not in the same way, of course. Maybe in the same way. Hell, I don't know. Even though our ages are closer than that of mine and D.B.'s, I refuse to find out in which way she sees me. It's a respect of boundaries, I think. At least that's what I'll go with.

She still looks at D.B., or as she calls him always by his full name Danny Boyle with her fading brogue, forever as a small boy playing in the fields behind a home back in Ireland where he never lived. Her courtesy toward the rest of the band surpasses motherhood into a friendliness of sorts. She well knows that the image they project is just that, an image. And after our introduction, she knew I was there to help them with that. The appearance. The words. The sound. The publicity. It's what I do, and more if needed.

I think the other reason nothing could ever happen is D.B. Respect for my client aside, the guy is enormous. Not fat, not orca fat, or that. I mean meat and potatoes, benches 425, bar room brawl champion big. The guy that never needed an ID to get into a bar. Here is a guy that got arrested one time, no stereotypes, for public drunkenness, and it took six cops and two tasers to take him down. While there may have been added strength because of the liquid courage, it wasn't much. I'm not afraid to fight, start a conflict if I need to. It's part of my job. Sometimes. Spurs creativity. But pick your battles. D.B. is a guy you want on your side, not a guy you go toe to toe with. Even if he was a guy to go toe to toe with, I'm more of a lover—less fighter, given a choice.

But bright, fire red hair since infancy—Eileen showed pictures like a proud mom. She carries a few in her purse like a small photo album. Sentimental reasons I assume. For D.B., the picture show was almost embarrassing, but it gave me a moment to be close to such beauty. And being close to raw beauty is where creativity is born.

I think Eileen is the sort of woman I could picture myself with, had life turned out differently. If I chose other roads, other options. Made different decisions. I would have loved to grow old with someone like her. But looking back on wouldas, couldas, shouldas doesn't help anyone, especially not the person doing the pondering. So, I appreciate her and her beauty at face value.

Back to our conversation though, yeah, I was down for a few. Maybe more. It's why I called D.B. He's not only a good client but one hell of a wingman. If nookie is what I need, this guy will help me land it with minimal effort. Not that I can't bring it in on my own. I can. I don't know many people who can't. But when the mojo is gone, it's gone, and getting all the help I can is much appreciated.

Grabbing drinks with D.B. is always an event. Sure, I get recognized sometimes. I have my moments when a lady, man, or person walks up to me and pays their respects. But I've faded from the spotlight. My time in it is over. I'm okay with that. I've had my fun with it. I've enjoyed the daily conversations with strangers about myself. The kisses from random women who wanted to be close to a star. I also grew to loathe it, getting to a point where going out was dreadful because I wanted to be left alone. Not that hordes of people were rushing me like screaming Usher fans, but there is always that one person who has to say something to you. It's never the guy who can just say,

"I'm a big fan," and walk away. It's the guy who needs to dominate your time for a half hour while you are holding ice cream you just pulled from the freezer case while grocery shopping. Nowadays, I don't mind it so much. Most of the time when I get recognized, it's a silent nod of recognition, a quick autograph, or a handshake. So goes the life of a producer. Leave the spotlight to those wanting the lime hue overtones, for those wishing to be seen. Leaving the spotlight is good like that.

In the public's eye, out of sight, out of mind—unless I'm with D.B. Three albums, all gold, still looking for their platinum. Three. I want to help them get their platinum. So anywhere he goes, he plays the rock star. He still craves the attention, the uncertain and exciting feeling of an ever-changing entourage, the ladies he meets, especially the ladies, oohing and ahhing over every little thing he says, like musical scripture and infallible idioms are spewing forth from his mouth. In short, drinking with this guy is always an event.

It's dark by the time I finish my ten-mile drive into Kissimmee to get there, which means the daily thunderstorm has already passed. If you've never lived in Florida, it's strange to experience the first time. You'll be driving, walking, whatever. You'll see gray clouds overhead, but that's it. Then, out of nowhere, it starts. Light rain. You think to yourself, *This isn't so bad.* But no sooner do you finish that thought than the light rain turns into a torrential downpour that reduces vision to a few feet. Your thoughts turn to panic mode as you slow down your driving or find shelter from the rain if you were unlucky enough to be walking when it started. You think to yourself, *Did I miss the news? Is this how hurricanes start?* But as you finally grasp hold of the situation, it stops. A light, barely noticeable drizzle.

The first time it happens, you can't help but wonder what just transpired. As if some Cthulhuian portal just opened up and the gargantuan mass of glowing orbs and eyes known as Yog-Sothoth is making its way through to devour us all. But no, that's just a standard three o'clock shower in Florida. It gives the humidity time to settle by nightfall. Now there are enough people here for the pre-hurricane-party party. Yes, the hurricane parties have begun. And yes, in Florida hurricane parties are a thing.

As befitting a rock star, D.B. has commandeered the patio section of our usual day-of-the-week-fried-food-two-hundred-grams-of-fat-per-entree-over-priced-restaurant we meet up at. The late nineties music flows softly from the sad excuse of a sound system, whispering below the mixed noise of conversations. Two of D.B.'s bandmates, Vincent and Neil, brown acoustic guitars in hands, strum a modern-day rendition of Simon & Garfunkel's "A Most Peculiar Man" while the females swoon around them as if this is the first time they have ever witnessed such musicianship. I'm not saying Simon and Garfunkel aren't musical geniuses; they are. But these chicks are either feigning newfound awe and amazement to get close to the band, or they need to listen to better music. D.B., complete with his signature, frayed, dark gray golfer's cap, leather wristbands, torn jeans, and Spear

Fist T-shirt, is in the center of a circle with everyone's attention on him—for he is the star of the show.

Sitting atop the back of an outdoor, woven plastic, black couch with red cushions, he makes a grand he-ho gesture and lets out a laugh, beer in hand, spilling a few drops as he does. The crowd follows suit, making me wonder how many understood the humor and how many laughed to avoid falling out of his good graces; as if he gave a crap about people who only care about him because of his money from music laughing at every joke. Half of these clowns could never see him again and he'd be no worse off. He has feelings of his own, but I doubt if anyone here cares much about those. He is human, after all, and (as The Smiths alluded to so many years ago) he needs to be loved, just like everyone else.

I enter the patio through the welded metal, waist-high swinging door. D.B.'s attention, and thus the attention of everyone surrounding him, turns to me. He sets down his beer as he stands and strides over. As much as he is into his nu-metal, rock 'n roll, bad-boy image, he'll always do the handshake into the one-armed hug with certain people. I'm glad in the short duration of our relationship I've made that list. It's always nice to see a friendly face in a strange town.

I've met some people in the few months I've been down here, people outside of clients, but they are all still strangers to me. People I've met through clients. Single-serving friends who want to hear every word I have to say but offer little to nothing in exchange. People sure are strange when you're a stranger. It's just a relief to see a friendly face.

"Finn!" His excitement turns to a quieter tone I know is meant only for my ears. "Thank the gods you're here, man. These people tonight! I tell ya."

I smile. Having been in his shoes before, I feel his pain of false friendships and passing acquaintances. "Nice to see you too, D.B. What's on the menu?"

As if in some Soviet-Era spy vs. spy game of espionage, his finger gestures to the crowd of Lt. Dans that moments ago were gathered around him and still eagerly await his, or the suburban's, return.

"A redhead I think you'll dig. Dyn-o-mite in the sack. Great head…" D.B. hesitates on something.

So, I chime in, "What's the but?"

He tries to hold in his words, "Strange amount of … long nipple hair."

I think the twisted face I make (that, in my mind, is a frightening version of the famous Reese Witherspoon face from the car ride scene in *Cruel Intentions*) says it all for him. He laughs a quiet laugh of understanding and continues. He eyes a gal sitting two to her left. She is turned away from me at this moment. All I see is long, black curly hair. It brings me back to my first night outside that greasy spoon of a hamburger-and-fry stand. I can't see her arm, tattooed in all its superhero glory. I can't even see her face as she talks to some Harley Quinn wannabe who stands, staring at me. She is cute, but at this moment, those eyes pierce into my mind again. Haunting me of a distant memory from better times never had.

"The one staring at you is an actual fan of yours. When I told her you were coming tonight, she stuck around just to meet you. No tricks there. She just wants to say her graces."

D.B. says these words and I hear them, but they are distant. Faded into the background of the moment while I try to send mental messages to this raven-haired woman to turn around toward me so I can see if she is the same woman who has been haunting my dreams of late.

"But the girl sitting with her back to us," D.B. says this and the volume of his voice shoots to the foreground of my senses, as if nothing else around is of consequence.

"Yeah!!" I respond, reverting to a sixth-grade schoolboy version of myself about to see his first set of real-life boobs. My heart races so fast and beats so hard, I feel a Death Star-size explosion coming on.

"She's the catch of the day if you can reel her in. She's been chatting up that girl she's talking to all night."

"What's her name?" I ask, nodding at what could be either lady. The Harley-esque one I meant to nod at notices me and smiles. It worked.

"Her? Vivian." He corrects himself, "Viv."

"The other? The black curly hair?"

"Jeanine."

He says it softly, but she turns around to glance at us as though she heard him whisper her name. My racing heart comes to a dead stop. Not in the butter-flies-in-the-stomach way you felt when you first fon-dled a pair of breasts back in grade school. No. This moment is a heart-stopping, loss-of-a-beloved-pet way. The way I felt when Lt. Dan was too old to move, too decrepit to enjoy any aspect of life, and had to put him to his final rest. That pain, or something close to it, is what I am feeling right now, at this moment. Her eyes have no fleck. They aren't hazel. They are brown. Her nose is not the same characteristic, Romanesque nose. The nose on her is small and cute, which is nice but lacks character. Freckles, yes. Not nearly as many or as nicely laid out. More crowded, larger freckles that make you think she had a rough childhood in school before the boys figured out the meaning of life. The sadness at this moment is harsh. I stare at a loss, even though there was never a win that could have occurred.

D.B. sees me staring past the night's options into the void of disappointment. He nudges me. "You okay?"

"Yeah. Just thought I knew her."

I look around and my attention is anything but focused. I again see the guitar players making sweet love to the dark wood Ibanez acoustics and their harem. The numerous other small conversations that go on around me. A fire lit in a fire pit, always a necessity at 75 degrees. I shake my head clear and turn back to my momentary savior.

"I need a drink."

"No worries, my friend. I already have one waiting. Shanghai Tea. As you always."

He knows me so well. I smile a half-cocked smile and nod an appreciative nod. We walk back to his circle and, like a trophy awaiting its champion, my beautiful, translucent green drink sits. As I pick it up, I watch the alcohols swirling about, mingling with the green liquor and rocks. A party in a glass. I take a sip and the party is now in my mouth. A sweet, pleasant, refreshing sip of alcoholic goodness that is a Shanghai Tea.

A quick note in case you've never heard of one: one part each gin, vodka, rum, and Triple Sec. Fill with sour mix, sweet & sour mix, whatever. Then top with a splash or two of Midori. It gives it the beautiful green color and a flavor like no other. That said, I am drinking my libation. The sip hits my tongue, and I am savoring the taste. I have to enjoy any small win I can to get my head in the game. Knowing that a woman named Viv wants to meet me helps with that.

After enjoying a moment to myself with my drink, I look at Viv. She is already trying to make eye contact. Not like a desperate barfly looking for love in all the wrong places, just casual. Her head is tilted down a tad. A slight, forced smile on her thin lips. Her long, blonde hair lends a view to the deep red-and-blue peekaboos underneath. She wears these black rim glasses that give her a look somewhere between a sexy librarian and a goth chick, both ready to tear your clothes off and rock your world while simultaneously having a most intellectually stimulating conversation with you. I figure tonight I'd be down for either, or both. Her blue-gray eyes stare into mine, waiting for me to make a move, to say something. But at this moment, I notice the Van Halen T-shirt she wears under an open plaid button-down. I smile at seeing her because her shirt makes me know that tonight, at least, she "Ain't Talkin' 'Bout Love." I nudge D.B. on the arm, a signal amongst men that a move is about to be made. And it is. I make a casual move closer to her, nothing that will be mistaken for the up-turned collar, wild and crazy guy or anything else.

"D.B. says your name is Viv." I find my spot standing next to the patio couch they are squatting on.

In my impeccable timing, I say this as she takes a sip of some blue-red cocktail that matches her hiding hair. She hurries her sip, a little spilling out of her straw as she does. She wipes her lips; it is an adorable gesture that makes me chuckle.

"It is. Oh, God." Viv stands up as if some big bomb will need to be dodged. "What else did he say about me?" Her face scrunches, unsure if she should already be embarrassed.

"Just that you were a rabid fan who has been stalking me for a while. Pictures, shrine, incense: the whole nine yards."

She laughs. Her ability to discern dry sarcasm from true sincerity is a welcome sign. The sigh of relief in her laugh relaxes her as she takes another sip. This time without spilling.

"It's all true. Many, many posters and pictures." She laughs and smiles a real smile.

"I assume your face has been cut out of other pictures and taped next to mine," I retort.

"Yes, all of my pictures have us together," she adds.

Then, before things can get awkward, she downshifts the tone with the smoothness of a pro racecar driver. "But seriously, I do own all your work. My absolute favorite stuff."

How else can I respond to such a gracious comment but "Thank you. It means a lot."

From the couch, Jeanine looks up at me. She cocks her head just a sliver to the side, as if a thought has entered her mind and she's not sure if it should be there or not.

"I know you," Jeanine interrupts us. A quizzical look is painted on her face at me, "Knew you."

"I've been on the radio once or twice." I'm not exactly sure how to respond.

"No. Like, actually knew you. You knew my mom." A statement that made a subtle, borderline standard moment shift past awkward to just short of uncomfortable.

"I've known a lot of moms. Dads too. Sisters, brothers..." I respond, not exactly sure where she's going with this.

"Holy shit! Tricky Finn?!" She says this and the world around me closes in. I can feel the physical shift of my pupils contract. From all angles of my peripheral vision, a black wave closes in and shuts out everything except for her. All noise around seems to cease. It's still there, I know it is, but my ears have stopped functioning. All I can hear is the sound of the blood rushing through dilated vessels of my inner ear and the pounding of my heart beating in my chest. And a high-pitched buzz that sometimes lingers like a bad hangover.

I want to collapse. I want to crash to the ground and let the world fade away. For the first time in my 38 years of existence, my body is incapable of functioning. All systems are at a loss on how to operate. Ceased. Breathing has stopped. I mentally have to force myself to breathe. Much more difficult than you could imagine. Speech is turned off. All systems are no-go. The moment paralyzes me. Those haunting eyes enter my mind and stab me right through my cerebral cortex (or whatever part of the brain controls function), making me unable to move. Those haunting, beautiful eyes with a brilliant fleck, the Roman nose. The freckles. All thrown off because of black number 1 hair dye, a curling iron, makeup, and a tattoo sleeve.

I think I feel a tear rolling down my right eye. I'm not sure. I try to move my hand, but it won't budge. Stuck. Stuck in this moment and unable to move as my mind scrambles to comprehend what is going on at this moment in my life.

This woman that sits in front of me, a woman I thought I didn't know. A woman I don't know, at least not anymore, knows me. Well, knew me. And it's because this woman in front of me knows me, I now understand why those eyes have been haunting me. Now my ears hear what she said as the emasculated man on the Vomatron was screaming like a little girl: "Faith," as in "You gotta have faith."

Why didn't it register that night? Damn that screaming, girly man.

It was her name. It was also a message; a message that dated back two decades or so to my first year of college. The flood doors have opened and all these memories come flooding in, a torrent of memories out of chronology hitting my optic nerve. They all flash: so random, so fast, so overwhelming. I need to sit. But I still can't move.

Faith.

CHAPTER 3

Sidedish Friend

*S*he was the only one to call me Tricky Finn; it was a reference to a singular event. Almost meaningless. Except that the name stuck. For Faith. This woman in front of me was not Faith. Faith was the love with whom I spent four years. She was the love that drove me insane like no other, that pushed me to try harder than no other, that inspired me to write more than any other, that inspired me to create better than any other. Everything I did, I did better because of her. She was my muse—my reason for leaving Chicago behind after college and moving to New York.

The first thing I remember from our introductory night together was the candlelight, the stereo softly playing Dave Matthews' "Say Goodbye." Soft sheets. So extraordinarily comfortable that I almost made mention of it, almost. The way she looked as she raised her arms, and I took off her top. The look in her eyes as she took off mine. I held the back of her head with my left hand as we deeply kissed. Tongues tangled around one another. Lips silently speaking to each other. My other hand reached for her bra clasp. She hesitated for a moment. I stopped. The night was for her, not me. We continued to kiss, and she nodded her head. Yes! My middle and index finger snapped against my thumb, clasp between them. It sprung open. Her breasts joined us as willing participants in that night's rendition of The Drunken Match Game.

Now her breasts were there, opened and on display. I did what all men do. I stopped and took a moment to admire. They were beautiful. Not ordinary. Marvelous. Magnificent. Greek wars scribed by Homer would have been fought over these breasts. Arabian Nights legends could have been written about just the beauty of the areola and nipple. That night, she chose to share them with me. She decided to share herself with me. I don't think a hot, fat child in hell getting a gigantic bowl of cold ice-cream could have been happier. And she knew it. The shit-eating grin on my face said it all.

Now, if you want your life to change, do something different. Not extreme. No skydiving, bungee-jumping, or anything like that. I'm sure it's fun and all. But I'm talking subtly different from your everyday. The events that led to the candlelit Dave Matthews incident only took place because of a poetry class. Class registration began at some ungodly early hour, and I knew if I went to bed, I'd never wake up on time, so I stayed up all night. I had help staying up thanks to Anastasia in 304, but I stayed up. Registration was during the start of finals week at the end of the first trimester. All this *seems pretty mundane but staying up without sleep let some bug I was harboring run rampant, making me god-awful ill. I lost forty pounds. I didn't mind that since I gained the freshman fifteen, so I was looking pretty good after my flu. Nothing big. Just a bad flu bug. But that's why I remember signing up for this class.*

It was some poetry class about war's refugees. As a musician, I thought the topic was, as I put it back then, dope. I needed an elective, and I figured this class might give me some insight, some inspiration, some way of looking at things I'd previously missed or overlooked. I didn't know it then, but I was using the biggest hammer around to hit the nail smack on the head. I just thought I might get a couple of sweet lyrical sets out of it. Instead, I found her. The nail the hammer was hitting had nothing to do with the class, of course.

To know where the following is coming from, the time is important. The era. The feeling of the decade. Saddam was still at the height of his power. Corporations were frantically starting to prepare for what could be the downfall of society, Y2K. We all know what a joke that ended up being. It was the last of the feel-good times of the eighties that trickled into and lasted throughout—though being horribly twisted by—the '90s. The end of the millennium. Political turmoil was brewing, as it always does on some level. Social values were shifting, which of course the older crowd was pushing back against. But we were going to be heard, as every generation will be heard, even if we had no clue what we were saying!

SIDEDISH FRIEND

The class itself was okay. The instructor was some renegade, a gray-haired priest who had multiple warrants out for his arrest from decades-old swords to plowshares protests (which he was all high and mighty about). All the students were soaking in every word he was saying like it was scripture. All I could think about was the pay he was getting at this Chicago, Catholic university. Where was his vow of poverty? Or did the renegade part allow him the luxury of money? Either way, something seemed off to me about him, but the rest of the students soaked up the rays of sunshine he seemed to illuminate. The skeptic in me couldn't help wondering if he had soaked up altar boys back in his day like these students are soaking him up now. Maybe it was the cynic in me.

For the first couple sessions, I was the Judd Nelson in the leather jacket. Daydreaming out the window, writing poetry while the teacher taught:

I sit watching the leaves fall from the trees
Listening to the crackling sound as they hit
the building
While in the background is the ambient talking of
the teacher.
I realize as we sit, 42 individuals, all being taught
the same thing
Becoming unconsciously institutionalized, that
Will was right
"They may take our lives... but they can never take
our freedom."

That was a real crap bag right there, first one from the class. The cynicism may have been dripping off my chin, but all that was about to be challenged. He gave us an assignment. Write a poem. That was it. So, of course, he got the barrage of zombified hands waving around, about to fall off dare they stop moving. All were asking questions in the same vein. "Write about what?" And like any good writer of any genre knows: write what you know. But these weren't good writers. Those students were only in that class for elective purposes. The same reason I was there I guess, but I was too holier-than-thou to see it back then. I thought I was too good for these other students. Figured everything I wrote was going to be gold.

I never liked writing songs directly about myself. I enjoyed making them a bit more worldly. Political. Lovely. Fantastical. Whatever the case. Not as introspective as Father Renegade Lorenzo Lamas may have wanted. So, the next class, I came in with my sarcastic, cynical look at America. Some would have said it was unpatriotic. Some said it was misogynistic and, therefore, I must have been. I just wrote what I saw.

The Dirt Will Climb

I love America and rightly so.
Only in this country can women be raped
And still men rule.
I love America and rightly so.
I see indifference grow,
Hate and love diminish
Hateandlovediminish.

SIDEDISH FRIEND

America is loved for what it stands for:
Freedom, Equality, Happiness
All for the upper class…
The upper ass…
Yeah, up your ass.
Women raped and children die.
This isn't freedom.
This is free dumb.
Just beneath the surface.
It's there you'll find
Dirt and slime, scum and grime.
The dirt will climb on cum and grime
But we should love our country…
God has blessed her…
We have blessed her…
We have caressed her…
I love America and rightly so…
Only in this country have I seen such change
To take segregation toward integration
And make it right…
Make it white…
We sing our song.
The right becomes wrong.
Follow along.
It's all so wrong,
But still, we love America.
I love America.
Burton loves America.

*Now the last line was a direct reference to a Fear
Factory song "Big God/Raped Souls," to which Burton
C. Bell does lead vocals. The song starts with sad*

statistics on American violence, especially such acts perpetrated against women. And finishes with an ironic declaration of love for the country. I assume it's a lash out against those whose morals are in direct contradiction of their actions.

So, the whole poem was inspired by what I saw in life, in the news, and that opening to the song, which I had only heard once before while in a client's old red Trans Am getting double meat Chorizo burritos from this old Chicagoland joint called El Famous Burrito.

"The Dirt Will Climb" was my vocal introduction to the class. While it didn't have quite the introductory impact of a nursery rhyme and baseball bat upside the head as I would have liked, it was still enough. I figured it would piss off a few people, make others think, and stir up some thought, discussion, and controversy, which is precisely what the class needed. Get these dead brains thinking.

That's just what it did.

The next class session we, of course, had to write other poems. I chose stoic silence this time around. Wanted to give someone else the chance to stir the cauldron of our minds. And one did. This stick-straight, dishwater blonde with freckles on a makeup-free face and a fleck in her left eye, wearing an earth-tone flannel shirt and fitted, faded jeans, who had been quietly sitting in a window seat, decided to pipe up. She straightened herself up, as if she was ever that slouched to begin with, cleared her throat while getting her poem, neatly printed on computer paper, out from her blue folder, and stared at me. A look in her eye that said,

"This poem is for you. You fucking douchebag of a man. Scum of the earth. Here's looking at you, shithead."

She then proceeded to read off this poem about being a woman. How hard it was to be female. Growing up middle America, some sect upper class, big city suburbs because once a month she bled for a few days. And oh, the pains of it all. How my eyes rolled. How everyone's eyes rolled. Yes, she saw my eyes point toward the ceiling, and it made her read her self-sacrificial poem all the more intensely, like someone-at a microphone-doing an open jam-slam poetry night-encircled by wreaths of smoke-while reciting what sounds like-every other-fucking-spoken-word-poem-where every-other word-is stressed-and thus-the meaning-of the poem-is lost-unlike Frost. Or Kerouac. Or Angelou. Or even Silverstein.

But she finished. And the class applauded its forced applause, and I applauded because she tried to write and however amateur, flat, or contrived the poem may have been, there was real emotion in her voice. Real feelings seeped out of her pores, and they were not encircling her like a wreath. Oh no. They shot at me, the poison-tipped arrows they were, trying to take me down with each shot. But I remained standing, well, seated. Alive. Her words could never hurt me. No one cared about the struggles of being a spoiled girl from a well-to-do house where nothing dreadful had ever happened. There were no real struggles.

I was a grade-A asshole back then. Sure, she may have called me out on it, but perhaps that's why I ended up doing what I did—Because she called me out. The beginning of the bettering of Finn Fairlane all started with this one incident. Perhaps.

The class let out thirty or so minutes later, and we all rose and hastily exited. I rushed out. One of the firsts. I didn't feel like being told off by someone who knew I thought lowly of their work. But I know I wasn't alone in how I felt because other classmates and I talked about it and her and whatever comments may have been told that I can't remember now, looking back. But I knew what I had to do.

For my next assignment, I wrote this poem called "I Will Build My Cross," and it was formatted to look like a cross. The poem itself was about individuals' exceptional ability to martyr themselves for any small cause just to garner attention while sweeping important issues under the rug of martyrdom. And yes, it was all aimed at her. While I read each line of what I thought was a poignant poem, her eyes stabbing deeper and deeper into my soul, trying to rip apart my heart, I knew she felt it. And the class ate it up. The round of applause I received was an unspoken thank-you from every other student for writing that poem for her. But no wars were going to start there. The applause was it. We read more poetry for the rest of the class and mine was seemingly left wayside.

The class ended for the day and I left. No war cries or rallies from the other side. No small group discussion was held dissecting line after line and how it fed on her poem. The round of applause was to be the end.

I opened the door to the outside world of wind screaming through the trees and whipping leaves.

The crisp, late autumn breeze hit my face with a sharp sting. It also could have been the over-sized pebble that hit square against my cheek, sending a cool pain spreading throughout the right side of my face. As I said, her words could never hurt me… but sticks and stones on the other hand.

A voice called out. Screaming. Shaking. Mad. It called out to me, and I knew it. "Asshole!" When someone speaks that word to you, you know it. It doesn't matter if you've ever heard that voice or not. The letters scream your name. My name may be spelled F-I-N-N, but at that moment it was pronounced, "Asshole."

I rubbed the side of my face with my hand and smiled through the minor, but annoying, pain.

"Did you rush out here after class just to ambush me?" I was searching for a wittier repartee, but the pain was blocking intelligent thought.

"Yes. No." She paused for a split moment, unsure of her actions as if she didn't know why she assaulted me. "I did. But not to throw a rock at your face. You're an asshole. You know that? A real asshole."

"So, I've been told."

"Well, you are. I'm not a writer. I'm taking this class because I thought it would be fun. Different. A break from business courses. Then you have to go and ruin it for me." The anger in her voice was fierce. Fiery. The wind blew her dishwater hair across her face, rhythmically whipping it with the fury in her words in vicious prose.

"Tell me how you really feel." As those words escaped past my teeth, I felt a shit-eating grin take over my lips.

"You sit in the back of the class all quiet and brooding. Not talking, not making friends. People talk. You seem interesting. Somehow, in a university of 14,000, you have a reputation. But you make yourself unapproachable. You think what I wrote was somehow self-righteous martyrdom?! Take a look at yourself."

I couldn't tell if she was angry anymore or just yelling to yell, but the passersby were watching, and she was so beautiful at that moment that I was just happy she was talking—yelling—at me and not anyone else. The hair blew across her face as she continually tried to move it back, as if the wind would listen to her pleas and calm down. The furrowed brow that crinkled her nose as she said I, "seem interesting." She didn't want to be mad. She just was. I'm sure the shit-eating grin on my face did nothing to quell the anger and frustration inside her. But I couldn't help it. She was beautiful in her passion. And I loved that moment. I loved her at that moment.

"Can I buy you a coffee or a drink or something?" I asked, hoping she didn't honestly want to be mad.

"What?" The surprised look on her face, unsure how to respond.

"Coffee, a latte, a margarita. I'm thirsty." Now I was just trying to break the tension. The passersby had all stopped spectating, and the scene had returned to normal. Students walked up and down the sidewalks. Leaves blew on the ground from the wind. Cars drove up and down the street.

Something in her had also returned to normal. Her breathing had slowed, and her brow un-furrowed. She looked at me, unsure of my intentions.

I pulled out a pack of red-and-white boxed ciga-rettes and flicked my wrist, so one flew out into my lips. I extended it in her direction, and she accepted with a raised brow.

A sounding relief in her voice as she told me, "Margaritas sound great."

Glad to have gotten that all out. It was that moment. Third trimester of my freshman year for which I was waiting. For whatever reason, my college was done in trimesters for the year, not semesters. Stupid, I know. But that's private schools for you. Nothing before that day seemed important anymore. I didn't know where this might lead. A drink with a stranger that never crosses your path again, or something more. But the magic in that moment of all her yelling in the chilly winds had sappy romance songs playing in my head. I was living out my very own teen romance flick and didn't care how cliché it looked.

"I know a place that doesn't card. Come on."

We started walking down Fullerton Avenue along the row of (possibly Victorian) townhomes that deco-rated the southern side of the street, a nice contrast to the apartments on the opposite side. It was not as awkward a walk as one might think. Looking back on it, one might say it was almost pleasant.

"Fairlane. Finn Fairlane." I went for the understated Bond introduction.

"Yeah, got that from class," was her reply.

I smiled a bit. "I know, but we never had a formal introduction. So, I figured."

She retorted, "Oh, I caught the gesture. Just don't think you're getting off that easy."

"But I don't know your name," I replied. Honestly, I didn't. Never paid attention really to people outside my circle. I guess wanting to know her name was my attempt at expanding that circle.

"Siubhal. Faith Siubhal."

She was beautiful and mesmerizing, and I wanted her to be mine. There was a hypnotic tone in the way she spoke. Very sexy. I had to play it cool and make sure not to overplay my hand. We already got off to one bad start. They say you never get a second chance to make a first impression. Logically, that is true, but if there ever was a chance this was it.

The icy feel of frozen watermelon margaritas hitting her taste buds was just what she needed. She relaxed deeper as the watermelon's smooth, calming voice echoed in her mind while slowly counting back. Ten... Deeper. Nine... That's it. Relax. Eight... Imagine steps. But her eyes were open. We were talking. She was from the suburbs but wanted to live on campus. Naperville area. I never much made it out that way before. Meeting her, wish I had.

She was telling me about her boyfriend halfway through our second pitcher. Maybe he was soon-to-be-ex, ex-something. Something about how he tried too hard to turn her into something she's not. She used to go to Scotland every summer with her family. Visit relatives. See the sights. But once she started dating whatever his name was, the trips stopped.

*He said establishing new roots was more important
than the past. Some lame crap, but she bought into
it. She had childhood dreams, as she called them, of
traveling the world. She wanted to go backpacking
through Europe. But no. She now thought living up to
the social expectations of landing a corporate job was
more important.*

*There was something in her voice, unsteadiness
or unsure, that made me not completely believe her.
Maybe it was the alcohol. Hell, the tequila made it a
bit difficult to concentrate and the more she drank,
the more she leaned forward. The more she leaned
forward, the more her cleavage popped out of her
top. While I tried to be a gentleman and not sneak a
peek, they were handcrafted by an artisan very close
to the creator, if not himself. And I was a tad bit ine-
briated. I continued to listen to her as she finished
talking about the inevitable demise of her latest relationship, all while sneaking peeks at her lovely bosom.
It looked such a place I wanted to fall into a deep sleep
on, after doing such activities that afterward require
a deep slumber.*

*"I honestly thought he was going to be the one I
spent my life with," she reflected on her naivete, "but
at fifteen, doesn't everyone think that?" She looked at
me for confirmation.*

*I nodded, if only to comfort her. There was no way
at fifteen I thought whatever girl I was with was the
one I was going to spend my life with. At fifteen, all
guys want to do is get their dong played with. Hell
at nineteen, twenty, twenty-five that's all we wanted.
Still, I nodded.*

"I wrote that poem you so wonderfully attacked as a way to deal with him." The truth comes out. *"He pissed me off. So many times. He always makes these promises but never follows through. Ya know? And he always has an excuse. For everything. It's like I'm only there for him when he needs. It wasn't always that way. He told me it would change come college, but I didn't listen. No! I am just his little…"*

"Were," I figured now would be a perfect time to interject.

"What?" She was stunned I spoke.

"You were just his whatever. Now you are your own, to be yourself. Find yourself. And do whatever you want," I finished that sentence as the last of the once frozen watermelon margaritas slid down my throat.

"Yes. You are right. You're such a good listener." She smiled.

"One of my many talents." I spoke as if I were some embodiment of a walking, sexual inuendo in her wilting world.

"Let's get outta here." The sinful grin on her face said what her words did not.

Which leads us back to her breasts, candlelight, and Dave Matthews on the stereo. I grabbed her, pulled her close to me. I wanted to meld our bodies together. So did she. She reached into my pants and said hello to my other half. She played around for a moment, exploring the newly discovered territory. Who was I to say no? But then she left. As quickly as she found this new land, filled with toys to play with, she evacuated the premises.

She took my hand and slipped it down her pants. Slid it down? Whatever. It was my turn to explore exotic, new lands. The anticipation was palpable as she piloted its crawling descent down. The feel of her soft skin as my hand made its way to the unexplored. But there were no jungles, no shrubs of any sort. She was smooth. Well groomed. And when a man internally compares in his mind how turned-on a female is to how hard he is, she was unmistakably turned on. These were wetlands. Florida Everglades waiting to turn into the Niagara Falls, excuse the geographic jump. As I slid my middle finger in, she quickly inhaled a short breath. A quick draw in that let me know I hit the right spot. I continued my spelunking adventure for only a few moments when she stopped kissing me. She gently pulled away from my hand. My finger slid out of her and her pants. My heart dropped. I figured this was it. Perhaps my talents were lacking, and she wasn't going to be my teacher. The ride ends here. Please exit to your left and have a great day!

She looked into my eyes for a moment. The abyss of my soul reached for her; she searched for herself in there. I stared back. A half-cocked smile broke on her face, and she leaned over to her nightstand. She opened the drawer, tossing me the holy grail of any first date.

"Put it on." Those were her words. Short, sweet, to the point. They were not a request. A demand. She knew what she wanted and for that night, at least, she wanted me.

She took her jeans off to reveal black lace panties, and the beauty of those lasted three point five seconds until she took those off as well.

So, I took off my jeans and put on my raincoat.

"I just want you to know, this wasn't my end game tonight." I was just adding for clarification. I realized I just sounded like almost every other female I had been with. A guy's version of, "I'm not normally like this." There, that night, it was true. I wasn't lying.

"Shut up. When a girl's ready, don't shut yourself out."

Yes, ma'am.

CHAPTER 4

The Devil's Dance Floor

"**A**re you okay?" Viv sees my thousand-yard stare into the past. Her words jab me, snapping me back to the present. I blink, shaking my memories from my mind.

There, in front of me, still sat Jeanine, a version of Faith that always pales by comparison. The annoying off-brand when the real thing isn't available. The irritating little sister who never failed to make her presence known: a fly at the picnic, a mosquito by the campfire.

"Yeah, sorry, Viv." I am trying to get my head into the night. I don't like disappointing fans. "It just so happens we're old acquaintances."

Jeanine looks down to take a drink as she shakes her head, a mixture of disappointment and unchanging expectations.

Viv looks to Jeanine for confirmation. "Something like that, yeah." Jeanine's dry reply could be served as a martini.

"Me and her sister used to be a thing. It was a long time ago." I hope she drops it.

"Hmm. You'll have to give me some details later." She takes no time in dashing my hopes.

"Perhaps." I leave it short and to the point.

Viv and I take a seat where we stood. Plop down on two red cushions in the dead center of a patio love seat. I somehow get maneuvered between Viv and Jeanine. I take a giant slurp that finishes off my Shanghai Tea. This irony here stares at me from both sides. And even though D.B. had no knowledge of my past with Jeanine's sister, he finds humor in something. He approaches with a new green savior of a drink in hand, laughing about something while nodding in my direction.

"Please join us," I beg of him as he hands me my drink. I notice the winds picking up. The palm leaves dance around wildly, playing air piano of some Rachmaninoff piece. The tiny lizards scurry about for shelter, lest they might get blown away. Even the little sparrows that usually keep company here, scavenging for food scraps, have abandoned us this night. A few early signs of the approaching hurricane.

"I see you're all getting along." D.B. settles back in across from me. A gust of wind tries to steal his golfer's cap, but he stops the would-be thief.

"Like old friends." The sarcasm drips off Jeanine's chin.

D.B. tosses a glance my direction, looking for clarification. I subtly shake my head no. Nodding his head, he drops it like a good friend.

"So," D.B. begins, "what ideas do you have in store for Badaboom?"

All heads turn to D.B. The minstrels stop strumming their guitars, giving the swooning companions a chance to scoot in a little closer. Conversations surrounding us hush down, waiting to hear something about the man or his band. Even the wind quiets for a moment before picking back up.

Viv chimes in, "What's ... Badaboom?"

"Their fourth album," I say. "Actually, plans for the record release party are coming along. The date's been finalized, which means we need to finish the opener. And the date is not as far off as you'd like."

"Did we get the amphitheater?" D.B asks.

"She couldn't book it, but I'm working on something" is my best reply.

Viv chimes in, "Anything you can tell us about the album?"

"Yes. Come to the record release party. The date is on their website. Enjoy live music, great beer, and good food." I pause for a moment as the crowd looks on. "The album, though, it's gonna be big, Badaboom. Spear Fist's best."

Heads turn to their cellphones to look up dates and conversations return to normal. The guitars are silent as the magic fingers of Neil and Vincent are now playfully flirting with the female fans who were so entranced moments earlier.

Viv turns her attention —and positioning —back to me. I take note and turn to her. D.B. notices, smiles, and nods approvingly. Caught up in the introduction earlier and the awkward moment of running into Jeanine, I didn't notice the small, jeweled bull ring she wears in her nose. Not my go-to cup of tea but she pulls it off nicely. A gracious accent on a smooth complexion.

Some person I've only seen around here a few times and whose name I have forgotten, if I ever knew it, sees D.B. sitting unattended to and saunters up to him. Normally this is not a noteworthy moment, except that this person has unknowingly caused D.B. to leave me to my own devices. No safety net for things that may go awry.

Christian: that's his name. Whatever —it doesn't matter. I have a beautiful lady sitting next to me.

"What is it you do for them?" Her first inquiry. I know she's just trying to make conversation, unsure of what to ask. Not wanting to sound like every other female who has sat in her seat, metaphorically speaking. But all fans sing the same basic praise, no matter how hard they try to stand apart. It's the nature of the beast. And it's okay. I never hold it against them. At least not the ones that look like her. She is just a fan wanting to talk.

"Not really sure how to explain it. I'm a producer of sorts." I try to keep it simple. Producer, writer, publicist, prodder: anything that helps the band stay motivated, inspired, and playing. In other words, doing their jobs. But musicians don't like that sort of stuff admitted about them, so I just say I'm a producer.

"I know what a producer does," she says, half offended.

"It's not a normal producer-musician relationship. I'm a muse. Sort of."

"You sort of amuse?" Viv's confused, almost embarrassed response by her misunderstanding was not masked. That's when I notice what makes her so beautiful, a mesmerizing sadness in her eyes. A driving need to never be wrong and then be ashamed when she is. A wondrous melancholy that makes her so enchanting.

"No. I'm a muse. Like those figures from Greek mythology who inspire creativity." I hope to eschew obfuscation.

"Weren't Greek muses all women?" she inquires.

"Now you know what I'm talking about." I smile.

"Now that my misunderstood wordplay has been clarified, yes." She smiles back. She might be smarter than I think.

"Yes, I believe they were all women, but it's the closest analogy I could think of." I want to move this conversation along.

"How does that work? Do you just show up, sit there, and they stare at you until they come up with something? Or is there more to it, I assume?" she jokes.

"Yes." I laugh. "There is more to it. I have my ideas as they have theirs. I take good ideas and make them great. I take great ideas and make them genius."

"Where do you get your inspiration from?" she asks as she puts her hand on my thigh. Her eyes connect with mine, and she gazes into them, a longing, lingering gaze that attempts to ensnare my soul. I dive back deep into her eyes, searching her soul. Looking for the roots of her sadness so that at least tonight, if only for a moment, I can take it away. Remove all of it and make her smile again. Smile like she did when I first made her feel relaxed.

I am just a man. And from her hand slowly creeping up my thigh, she wants to verify that. I am no longer mildly irritated by Spear Fist's two members, who have resumed their playing and are now strumming "Mrs. Robinson" for their fans. I suddenly find their music a perfect setting for tonight, even if I'm Mrs. Robinson and she's Dustin Hoffman's Ben Braddock.

"Where do I get my inspiration from?" I pause. Keeping eye contact, I put my hand on her hand. I just rest it there, not stopping her. Just letting her know that she has permission to continue.

"Yes, where do you?" Her coy words need no direct reply. She turns her hand to grab mine. She puts my hand on her thigh, just above the knee but slightly toward the inner side. An open door, if you will, to come in for a drink.

Perhaps it's the liquid courage from the green drinks instilling in me the confidence that Bruce Banner has in his strength when he's in Hulk form. Maybe it's the simplicity in the mood of the night air as the hurricane approaches. Perhaps it's the feeling of false impending doom of the hurricane that everyone is using as an excuse for the behavior of the evening. Or it's the simple answer I give, proving that sometimes genius doesn't have to be complicated or wordy—just stated.

"From moments like this." I hope the words I speak will let me see her good graces, as D.B. put it.

And they do. Viv leans in to kiss me but stops. She is inches away. I can smell her faded, sweet perfume. The smell of mixed liquor on her breath whispers to me that a kiss is waiting. She stops and pulls back. Scared, perhaps. Hesitant because of who I once was. Who I still may be in her eyes. A man who's written some songs, but as it begins, "a man." I am just a man. A man who wants her at this moment, as she wants me. So, I grab her hand and pull her toward me. We inch closer and closer together. Our eyes slowly close as our lips begin to touch. Such gentle, soft lips. She frees her hand from mine and places it high on my thigh. I, not wanting to leave my hands with nothing to do, put one on the small of her back and the other behind her head. Our tongues waltz around, enjoying the moment in their temporary homes.

She stops for a moment, not to pull away, but to gently bite my bottom lip. She tugs on it with her teeth, and it feels great. I open my eyes to find her looking into mine. We search the abyss of our souls. She lets go and runs her tongue across my bottom lip, as if to put it back in place. Her eyes swim up from the depths of where they just were and close. She kisses me again, no tongue but a deep kiss still. Perhaps more passionate than before. More enthusiasm and eager-ness in the performance.

She pulls back and opens her eyes again.

"Thank you," she says.

As if I did her a favor.

"No. Thank you." The only thing I can come up with. My mind has blanked; all wittiness is gone. I just look at Viv as any man would —with amazement —and with a longing for more. Maybe simplicity is the right word choice.

"Perhaps I'll see you again, Finn Fairlane." She stands up.

"That would be nice, Viv." An unsure response from a slightly confused man. I'm not used to a one-kiss wonder.

She turns and exits out the same swinging door I entered through, the loud clang of metal on metal as it hits against the frame. No one seems to notice. No one turns. At least not that I see, and if anyone did see, no one appears to give a crap. Down a sidewalk lined with parked cars facing her, she walks away with a confident sway in her hips. A happy swing with equal parts excitement. I watch as she disappears around the corner of the building. One last glance back to me and a not-so-subtle gesture with her finger that I should follow her.

I look around at all the people, too enthralled in what they are doing to have noticed her. The young gals too entranced by learning that heaven does hold a place for people who pray. Hey, hey. And I think I may be about to find out if heaven is a place somewhere on Earth—and know what it's worth. We could just do the deed right here. The others drink their martinis while waxing existential. At most, they would comment on the futility of the act. A few are merely comparing their just finished night at work. They might cheer us on but more for laughs than anything. I finish off my drink as I stand up, tapping D.B. on the shoulder. D.B. looks up, and I just give him a nod and a wink ... and my glass. He nods back, takes my empty drink, and raises his in a silent toast.

I step beyond the swing gate I entered through and turn the corner Viv ducked behind. I look around; she has seemingly disappeared. There's a bustle in the trees that line the back of the building. Not my hedgerow, so to speak, but I'm not alarmed. Tonight, I shall find my stairway.

I take a few suave steps to the trees, doing my best Ben Affleck a la *Good Will Hunting* bar scene, hoping she can see me. A little laugh lets me know she can. I make my way through the trees to her. Once I'm within arm's reach, she grabs my belt loops and pulls me toward her, not wasting any time.

"I wasn't sure you'd follow me." She wastes no time in unzipping my pants.

"If you walk away, I will follow." I paraphrase.

I look her in the eye while I say this. It was sincere, and I want it to come across that way. I want to see if I can remove some of that infinite sadness from behind her melancholy eyes, if only for a moment.

She smiles.

I move in, and our lips touch. Gently. Gliding over each other, waiting for the right moment to interlock. Something about this moment sent shivers down my spine. My hands reach around as Viv's back forms an involuntary arch at the touch of my fingertips. I slowly lift up her shirt to reach her bra clasp.

Her hands make their way up my shirt, knowing she has free range to explore my body. Perhaps a charade telling me what she wants me to do to her. I unclasp her bra. Her muscles quiver in anticipation of the coming moments. The realization of this delights me; for where else may my fingers excite?

Her breast fills my whole hand as it rests its glide over her chest. Soft-skinned and perfectly perky. Her nipples are hard and magnificent. I move my right hand to her jean button and start to undo it.

She pulls away, slightly. Even our lips stop caressing. The potential reasons are running through my head. *Are we done again? Bathroom break? Did she hear someone heading our way?* The list goes on and on and all in about 2.1 seconds.

I look her in the eye, waiting for her next move. She pierces me with not just her eyes, but her subtle smile too.

"I can't tonight." She frowns.

All my boyhood hopes go rushing out of my mind. Spewing forth at the wrong moment on a night of drinking, the drunkard's projectile vomit that is her words have hit me in the face, and I can taste the bitter saltiness of each of those three words. **I:** Bitter, a reminder of what Campari and all its crappiness taste like. The acidity of the single letter. **Can't:** Salt added to the mix of the moment. **Tonight:** The chunks of partially digested food covered in the previous. My only saving grace is that they are just words. No actual vomit to accompany them, but still, I want to scream to the skies above, "Why then! Why would she do this to me?! What have I done to her that she damns me so?!" But I remain calm.

"I understand" is the only calm reply I can utter, as my hands retreat from under her shirt.

"It happens," she responds with a scrunched look on her face that says it all.

"Usually about once a month," I retort, resting my hands on her waist.

She smiles and little laughs escapes her.

"Perhaps another time," I say, assuming this is the end.

She whispers coy words, "I never said we were done."

She grabs my belt loops again and lowers herself down. The fact that she grappled my belt loops twice tonight, each time with a single finger per loop, made me wonder if this was her move. Like John Cena waving his hand in front of his face, crowd chanting "You can't see me," before winning the match with his "Attitude Adjustment," she pulls on belt loops and does her thing.

As much as I'm a fan of Mr. Cena, the feel of Viv putting me in her mouth slingshots me back to this moment. No offense, John. The warmth. The wetness. The puppy-dog-look in her eyes that searches for approval as she peers up at me. I look down, smiling. I put my hand on the top of her head and let out a soft moan. She shuts her eyes and goes back to doing what she does. And man, does she do it well. The feeling of hitting the back of her throat as she takes me all in. The quiet moans she makes. A woman who truly enjoys her work.

The talent in this woman only takes a few minutes before both my hands are on her head. The sure sign that things are coming to a close. I am waiting for her to come up from the ground and tell me to finish elsewhere or to leave me blue-balled. But a true artisan of her work she is. She takes me all-in moaning just a bit louder, enough for me to feel the vibrations as I slide ever farther down her throat. With one hand, she cups the boys a final time. A gentle press of her fingers against them and that is it. She swallows every last bit of me, as the warm ecstasy of the moment washes over my body. Toes curl in my shoes. She looks up at me as she forces out the last drop. Licking the last of the batter off the tip of the beater, she stands up.

"I wore this shirt for a reason tonight. I'm glad you caught on." Her choice, whispered words to me as I zip up my pants.

"Happy to oblige." What else can I say? Blood flow has still not returned in full to my brain.

She steps out from behind the trees and I follow behind, the puppy dog I've become for the moment following my new master. She stops for a moment as my senses return. My world that was focused solely on her has widened, and I hear footsteps close behind me. We start to walk back to the patio as I turn my head to see who's approaching.

In the shadows of the parking lot lights, I see the unmistakable tribal ink on the arms of a torso too big for the legs that supported him at Old Town and are still too big to support his frame. I stop. I have become a deer frozen in headlights. Faith, standing next to him, eyeballing Viv up and down, hasn't noticed me yet.

"A cup of male tears for the lady. Nice." He attempts some form of brute-sophistication, a Neanderthal's version of calling out that he knows what just transpired.

I may not be the most mature man on the planet, but I do think I have a bit of decorum about me. My eyes squint a bit, and my nose furrows a little. My head tilts to the side and as I stare at him, trying to find the place in him that spews forth such audacious and crude things, then I see them: his oversized muscles.

Viv turns, sees me stopped in my tracks, and takes the few steps back to me. Faith and Viv make eye contact. Viv just smiles, knowing Faith is judging with condemnation in her eyes. Viv's "fuck all" attitude makes her more attractive at this moment. For all Viv cares, Faith could vanish out of existence, and all would be well. She has no idea of the full depth of our relationship, our past. Faith's eyes break contact with Viv, and for a fraction of a fraction of a second, my body floods with relief of the ending moment. Faith will walk right by and not even look at the man who defiled this lovely, carefree woman.

But no.

Faith's eyes move to me, the deer about to be slaughtered in her headlights. My mind in all its wisdom and glory shoots back to my first night here and remembers how it failed me. How I needed my mind to give me power beyond anything I've used before. How in that moment when I needed my mind the most, it failed me and let me fucking nod. My thoughts swim fast, knowing it must make up for that first night. Understanding, at this moment, I need something so strong, so powerful that no one will be able to retort back. She'll smile. All will be right in the world. And nothing awkward will happen. The overgrown behemoth will continue making caveman remarks. Viv will go back to the patio and have a good conversation with me. Faith and her little sister will talk and not bring up the past. And my mind delivers its redemption for past failure.

"Just finding some faith in Orlando," exits my mouth as she stares, possibly hoping for some growth and maturation from years gone by.

She stares, the look in her eyes of familiar disappointment. The three seconds they've been standing here feel like forever to me because in some parallel universe it has been forever.

"Let's get a beer," he says.

It's nice to know three seconds is his attention span. I knew this Neanderthal would help me out somehow.

Faith's attention shifts back to her man and she smiles, shaking off the moment.

She adds, "And a shot. Something strong."

He nods, and they walk off.

Viv stands next to me once again.

"I think I got all the details I needed." Viv motions to Faith and her man.

I just look into her eyes, searching for something to say. Viv is such a nice woman, and this night has gone so well.

"Look. We just met. You're nice, and your past is your past. I have a feeling that some of it is going to get dug up here tonight and I like the impression I have of you so..." Viv pauses mid-sentence.

My mind is racing on what is about to happen. It sprints back and forth in an empty room, searching for possible scenarios about to play out. But nothing pops up. It can't think of anything, good or bad.

She reaches into the front pocket of her flannel and grabs a pen. Viv has a receipt on which she writes down her number.

"So take this. And you'd better call me cause I had fun and want to do it again," she finishes.

Not the ending I thought was coming, but considering I couldn't think of any to begin with, I can't think of any better way it could end.

She leans in and kisses me one last time. I kiss her back for a moment, then she pulls away.

"Till next time." Her parting words as she walks to her car.

I stand for a moment watching, in awe of the events that transpired and the fact I got out dodging all bullets, for now. Viv enters a silver BMW and pulls away.

Good graces all right and graceful. I pocket the receipt and head back to the patio.

As I enter, D.B. turns to me and applauds. I smile a forced, modest smile, knowing damn well I want to soak in the cheer. I wave him off, but it only makes him clap louder. A few others from the crowd join in. While I'm unsure if they know why they are applauding or not, it doesn't help my situation at the moment. Faith and her giant take a seat next to Jeanine. Jeanine is leaned over, whispering in Faith's ear. She follows me with her eyes as I cop-a-squat by D.B.

D.B. tells me about something, but his voice is faded to the background. All I can do at this moment is sit, sip my watered-down drink that D.B. replenished while I was behind the trees, and stare at her. At Faith.

How did I miss her that first night? Yes, her hair is drastically different. Different color, different cut. Her arm is now adorned in splendid ink. A masterwork started and completed in the years gone by since our final college rendezvous. She does her makeup differently too. Hell, she wears makeup now. While I can rationalize the many, many things that have changed in the seventeen or so years since I last saw her, I still can't grasp the fact that I didn't recognize her.

She shoots a glance my way. D.B.'s voice rises to the foreground, and I hear him.

"You know what I mean?"

Crap. What a sentence to come back in on.

"Yeah" is all I can muster.

"Bro, you are so out of it right now. Still thinking about Viv?" His attempt to help me through whatever this moment is.

Shit. I had forgotten so soon; I didn't mean to. Viv seems like a pretty rad chick. But here I am, 21 again: stupid and naïve and indecisive. Wasting moments that cost me days. Wasting days that can cost me months if I'm not careful. And months into, well, you get the point.

The thing is the time between when Faith and I last saw each other and now, filled with the moments movies are made of. All those stories, as fun as they are, are not filled with real emotion, real meaning. It's all faceless sexual partners, countless drugs, and time forgotten to the hangover in between. Yes, it was fun. Yes, it made me who I am. A once glorious rockstar producer with a following enough to give me a big head for a few years, wreak havoc on my body, and ruin relationships. That time has passed. I've paid my dues and earned my respect in the industry. That's why I get my royalty checks and land the clients I land. But all those years—all those stories—they would never have happened if I had not been with Faith before. If I had not had a weight to carry on my back, a burden to bear, so to speak.

Here she is again. The universe is telling me something. I would say to myself to take this moment and shake it, come carpe diem baby, and go after her again. But the breathing metaphor of the roadblock between us is a bit much right now.

I look at D.B. I give a look that says it's time to take off the mask of rock star for a moment. His grin fades. "What's up?"

"You know your girl?" I'm not exactly sure how to tell him without telling him.

"Which one, Finn?" A slight cocky smile comes across his face.

"THE girl," I say.

"Yeah." The smile fades from his face once more.

He knows what I mean. Musicians, actors, entertainers: we all come to a choice at some point where we must choose, love or art. The great ones struggle against the love they left behind for the art that called to them, an obsession that holds them like a dangerous addiction. Then, of course, their art becomes a reflection of that love they left behind. The cocaine and alcohol-fueled pornucopias for which music is so well known. They are all just ways to drown the past.

The struggle against the tide and undercurrent that perpetually tries to pull us under.

So yeah. He knows. He knows all too well, too.

A slight head nod toward Faith is all I motion, and he now knows. Now he knows the whole story though no details were needed. He sees the face of my pain. The one who shaped me. The one I left behind, not that I had a choice.

But now I do.

I sit close enough to Faith, her man, and Jeanine. Figure I can work myself into a conversation somehow. Keep it casual. Maybe Faith has forgotten me. Maybe that night, when she said her name, I read too deep into it. Maybe that's been her move all along. A play on her name to lure guys in. Perhaps not; the stares she and her sister give me say I was anything but forgotten. Much like Napoleon, I'll just wait and see how this plays out.

So I'm sitting near them. D.B. is enjoying himself but keeping an eye on me. Watching. He might be as hopeful as me. He and his bandmates are the only other ones here who understand, who know what I feel and what I've been through to get here. But his bandmates have moved on to play "A Hazy Shade of Winter."

I sit and wait.

The machine of a man that is Faith's boyfriend extends a hand.

"Name's Ronnie," he says to me as I shake his hand. "Nice job behind the trees. From what I've heard, her BJs are the bomb."

Faith shakes her head.

At least he's not shy. I'm figuring, with his quick intro, he has no idea about Faith and me, our past. I also imagine a guy his age describing the sensual act that was her blowjob as "the bomb" isn't an intellectual equal. But at least he's friendly.

"We had a nice time. Name's Finn. Nice to meet you, Ronnie."

He gives me the look, the "are you him" look.

And he starts, "Are you…"

"Yes. I am, but let's keep that between us."

"Love your stuff, man. I've gotten laid to your music so many times," he says, his inner schoolboy coming out.

His words put a smile on my face. My eyes shoot toward Faith, knowing she's had sex while listening to my music after we were an us. Makes me feel warm and cozy inside knowing she's held on to something we once had.

She sees me, and from the slap on the arm she gives Ronnie, heard us too.

She glances between both of us. "It seemed a suitable way to defile us," she chimes in.

That was a perfect jab to two men. Respect.

"Whatever helps." Not my wittiest but it'll do.

Ronnie turns to Faith.

"Do you know who this is?" he asks her, a gleam in his eye.

"Yes, honey, I do. We went to college together," she says, hiding what she wants from Ronnie.

"Good times, I say," I respond.

"Damn, that must've been awesome. Knowing him as he makes it big." Ronnie is oblivious to life.

"They were something all right." She smirks.

"Something, yeah. I think they were fantastical," I shoot back.

Shit's getting real. And I see the ever-so-slight wrinkles of her furrowed brow she gets when she wants people to stop talking about whatever it is they are talking about.

"Honey," she says to Ronnie, in a tone of voice usually reserved for small children. "Why don't you go get us a drink?"

Ronnie stands and takes a step, but stops.

"What do you want?" His words ring earnest.

"Surprise me." Borderline irritation seeps through in Faith's response.

He turns to me. "You want somethin'?"

I shake my head. "No thanks."

He waddles inside, making a perfectly timed exit for us to continue.

"What are you doing here?" Faith cuts to the chase. I can tell the answer she wants is vacation, or just leaving, but it's not.

"He's polite, asking if I wanted something."

"Don't avoid the question." A demand I shall have to meet.

"Me? I live here. Moved down from NYC. Needed a change of scenery." I pause for a moment, making sure I won't have to eat my next words. She waits. "You look drastically different from back in the day." I shift subjects, hoping it lightens the mood.

"Time will do that to a girl." She cracks a smile.

"Time's been good to you." I smile back.

She stares into my eyes for a moment, searching for something. Perhaps the "why" of why I'm here, on this patio, tonight. Or why after all these years fate brings us together again. It could be a simple stare, injecting me with thoughts of her wanting me to leave—or jump off a bridge. I think the preceding smile means it's the former of my thoughts.

I continue, "How have you been?"

"How do I sum up seventeen years? Good. I guess. Still doing my thing," she summarizes, trying to figure out my intentions.

"And what is your thing, as of late?" I inquire. An ineffable need to know on my part.

"Makeup and cosmetology. The business world wasn't doing it for me anymore. Just needed a change. A better place to practice my brand of it. Florida worked. Art scene and all."

"I see. It works for many people, including myself."

Jeanine interrupts, "As fun as rehashing the tragedy of your past will inevitably be, I'm going in to keep Ronnie company. I'll drink your drink."

Jeanine stands up and starts toward the door.

"I'm sorry, sis. We could talk about something else." Faith reaches for words.

"No worries. You kids have fun. Just not my scene." Jeanine pierces me with a look that screams "beware."

"Nice seeing you again, Jeanine. We'll have to catch up." I try to sound honest.

"Yeah, like behind the trees? You wish," she smarts off, walking into the restaurant, leaving my face a pale shade of embarrassed red.

I turn back to Faith. Memories surge into my mind, a deluge filling every corner till it bursts through the top. I can't help but to think about how we started, how we loved, how we hated, how it all came to a halt. But as quickly as those thoughts came, she pulls me back in the harshest way.

"So a quickie behind the trees in a restaurant parking lot? A little passè, don't you think?"

"We didn't have sex." My mind is searching for a way to end this conversation. Grasping for anything to finish this before it goes further.

"You took a girl behind the trees and didn't nail her? Poor boy. What happened to your skills?" She delights in my misery just a little too much.

My mind wants to say anything to end this. And of course, it doles out the first thing it conjures up.

"She gave me some head. We couldn't boink."

She laughs, lightening the mood for the moment. "'Boink?' Did you just say boink?" It's nice to see her relaxing a tiny bit.

"I did. It was the first thing that came to mind." I shrug.

"Some things never change." She shakes her head.

I wait for her to continue that thought. I don't want to be the one to say it. She stares at me, maybe she's waiting for me to say it. But I can't. I won't.

And she continues, "That's not always a bad thing."

I smile, hoping for something. For anything.

"I didn't come here tonight to get back with you. We ended years ago. You made a choice," she reminds me.

Not what I was hoping for, but since I didn't know what I was hoping for, I guess I can't complain.

"You left me. You gave me no choice. But let's not do this again." A weak rebuttal on my part.

She holds back what she wants to say, to scream in my face. She laughs the laugh of someone who thinks they've never been wrong. That conceited, pretentious laugh of superiority, but I let her have it.

I wait. I'm not saying anything that can fuel the fire. Nothing that will make what minute progress we've made tonight fall further back.

She eyes me with cautious intent, wanting to say something new. But she holds out and looks at my face, not my eyes, but my face. Searching for a tell, for a twitch or jerk in my muscles that says, "I'm not really here, in this moment." But I stay still, wanting to hear what words she has to say.

"Coffee." Her one-word response to the standoff. Not nearly as tantamount to the evening as I thought it would be. But with Faith, one can never be too sure.

"You want me to get you coffee?"

"Ha." She forces the worded laugh. "Silly boy. Tomorrow evening, after I get off work. Coffee. A chance to catch up without Ronnie, Jeanine, or anyone around."

"Sounds good. Where?" I ask.

She stands up, ready to head in to see her man. "Coffee Shop of Horrors. 6:30."

"Word."

She nods and smiles before turning to step inside.

D.B. is staring at me, jaw agape at the miracle of me not getting slapped, punched, or stabbed but instead asked for coffee. A miracle it may be, but only time will tell. D.B. swigs from his drink. He wipes his mouth with his forearm.

"Bro. She's what led you here in the first place." He casts his warning in a sage-like way. Nothing cryptic. Just a matter of fact with the knowledge and experience to back it up.

"I know." My head hangs, as if this isn't going to be a good idea. Of course, it's not going to be a good idea. It's never a good idea. They say the definition of insanity is doing the same thing over and over, expecting different results. I'm just hoping I can change one variable to shift it to my favor. But sometimes it's better to let sleeping dogs lie. My thoughts once again turn to our past.

CHAPTER 5

Life Loves A Tragedy

*T*he college years were kind to us, or so I thought at the time. Looking back, not even the rose-colored glasses of time past can hide the tragedy that was Faith and Finn. Hell, even Tommy and Gina had a prayer to live on, which worked for them because years, later Mr. Bon Jovi informed everyone that they never did back down. If only Faith and I had built a stronger foundation.

That first night was everything a musician, a budding man, anyone really could ask for. Wild, intense, passionate. Romantic in its own way. It was fueled by desire and feelings that were, perhaps, new to both of us. Faith thought she hated me. Then next thing you know, I'm balls deep, pulling her hair, and smacking her ass. Maybe it was a hate fuck. I think we've all been in a situation where we either have or have wanted to screw someone out of our hatred for them. Perhaps that's what this started as for her. Perchance it was to spite her ex-boyfriend or whatever he actually was. No matter what her reasons for riding me like Slim Pickens waving his hat as he plummets to his doom on a nuclear bomb in Dr. Strangelove were, the fact that we did what we did changed our futures.

Had she not thrown the rock at me, had she just kept her hatred of my writing to herself, had I not been a pompous ass and written that poem in response to her, had what's-his-face not treated her the way he did to make her want to write the verse, had business classes not been such a bore that she needed to break the monotony with a left field elective, had any of those things and a million more not happened, we wouldn't have been in bed that night, losing ourselves in one another and forgetting our problems for a few moments.

What a great night for either point of view. I remember sometime in the early part of the nineties, the phrase "wild, passionate sex" was used all the time. The stupid conversations I'd have with friends about the phrase. We'd be laughing, trying to understand how something like passion, which is supposed to be a slow, candlelit romance, could be wild. Which, by definition, is anything but candlelit, unless you want to knock it over, starting wildfires in the Hollywood Hills. But that night was it. Wild. Passionate. What a grand description of our relationship. Wild it was. Worldview-changing.

After that night, things slowly went downward. We started something akin to an affair. College is a time for exploration. We both knew it, yet we were drawn to each other. We tried to make this aberration of a relationship we created work. There were regular accusations that flew around the room. The Mondays she would throw fists, accusing me of sleeping around. Even though the Friday before, she would tell me she needed time away and a break from us. A lot of accusations flew. Not all the time, mind you. Though when they did, the room was covered in a veritable Jackson Pollock wallpaper of shit from the fan, flinging it everywhere. It was disgustingly glorious that two people could be so passionate and angry with each other on such a level that we let things get to the depths, heights, level, whatever, that they did.

Then there was the passion. Romeo and Juliet could be so lucky. I always felt ours was more akin to Clarence and Alabama. If you don't get that reference, see True Romance, the most romantic love story ever told on film. Yes, I include Titanic in that. Titanic didn't have the to-the-ends-of-the-earth bond of love that True Romance had. Ours did. At least when it did, but don't we all hold onto the best parts of the past, the parts that don't hurt? The times that don't remind us of why we aren't still there, until we need to.

Yes. It started out rocky. Unsure of what really attracted Faith to me, of what drew me to her. Looks matter. Sure, they always do, and anyone who says otherwise is deluding themselves. No one is going to walk up to a person with open boils on their face, front teeth missing, and flies buzzing around their unwashed hair, snot dripping down their nose, thinking to themselves, Let me get on that 'cause they may have a glowing personality. So yes, looks matter. But there was something there more than looks. The ability for her to challenge me, for me to challenge her. To push each other to be better than we were. Always moving, redefining, pushing forward to better yourself, your being, and your art. Yes. It started out rocky, but it started out great. It started with a bang. No one wants a boring, uneventful relationship. And ours was not. Nights out on the town followed by great sex back at her place. Or mine. Sometimes we didn't even make it back there. Hell, once we were in an empty car on the "L" train late one night, coming back from somewhere downtown. We couldn't wait. Didn't want to wait. No, we didn't Risky Business it. But she went down. Like a goddess. And it was amazing.

But here's the thing: all those memories I have about great sex, great times with her, other things were going on, things that don't look so great.

Our first few months together was a casual thing. We weren't exclusive and didn't expect each other to be. I spent my time away from Faith working on music. Finding inspiration where I could, which meant a lot of different women. Don't get me wrong: she wasn't waiting around for me, twiddling her thumbs. She had her fun, too. Though I never inquired into what that may have entailed. It's not like I meant to sleep around. Things happen. It was college, and I was on a hot streak. I did meet a few chicks who inspired me to write a few songs. Some of which a few years later turned into Hot 100 Billboard songs: break-up songs, songs to have sex to, songs to drink on the beach to. But those gals, as inspiring as they were, were empty. They didn't hold any real meaning, but damn if it didn't help my art. And that's what mattered.

I remember this one chick who worked the front desk at my dorm. She was cute, innocent, smart, but still naïve enough to fall for the "I don't have game" game. Probably the only one I felt bad about hooking up with. Not that it wasn't consensual. It was, but there was this look in her eye when she told me she wasn't usually like this. In college, every female says that line. And every guy follows it up with either "I know" or "I can tell." Both of which were crocks of shit said to advance the porn playing out in the guy's mind that was manifesting in front of him. The same look when she asked me to call her that said she actually wanted me to. That said, she wasn't actually like this, that she was letting me into a world that not many hold sacred, that she didn't share with just anyone.

But here I was being let in. She didn't want me to disappoint her. The way her eyes lit up when I told her I would, and this wouldn't be just a one-night stand. It was the only time I felt bad after. That was the moment the realization solidified in my mind that I was the type of guy who became the reason people stopped holding their bodies sacred. Because guys like me would find a way to weasel ourselves in and defile their sacred dry lands by opening floodgates. And they wouldn't even feel bad about it till the next day—on their walk of shame back to their dorm rooms, not even breakfast money on the nightstand for them.

Nights like those happened. The people I met, we shared dreams, philosophies, ideas about life and death and love and war. What hopes have passed at such a young age and what dreams may come. What dreams the future may hold. Existential crap that then seemed so intense, so profound, when really we probably sounded like we were talking out our asses. I still have thoughts on existentialism and things more profound than the immediate. But back then, we were just figuring out life with the idea that we already knew it all ingrained in our heads. We were nineteen years old and just discovered the joy of our genitals only about six or seven years earlier.

But as the months went on and I added a few more notches on my belt, I came to a realization. I wanted more; more of what though, I didn't know. Just more. I felt like I was headed in the right direction. The only problem was I didn't know what direction I was heading in. I was lost at sea.

For about two months, I shut myself out for a bit. Just classes and music. I wrote. A lot. It was great. For me. Not a terribly long time in the big scheme of life. But to a college student during the school year, it was forever. To the woman I shut out, it may have been a little longer than that. I think in that time span, I was with Faith maybe four times. Maybe. I did make it a point to call her every day and talk. I wanted to stay close to her. I honestly did have feelings for her. She was not happy about the lack of time I had, though, but I was honing my art, perfecting my craft or some bullshit. But that's the mind of a creative soul. It never really changes.

Some time, I'd say in our third year of college, Faith noticed me starting to pull away. I didn't mean to. She was amazing. She was my best friend, my confidant and my partner in crime. She continued to push me to be better at my music, to be a better version *of myself, as I did her, in her own ways. But pushing can be construed as poking and prodding. No one likes being poked and prodded, at least not outside the bedroom.*

We got mean. The Friday/Monday accusations. Not every Friday, just the ones she let slip that she met a hot guy. So, I let her do her thing. But as I said, neither of us were waiting around the telephone for the other to call, all the while twiddling our thumbs. I was out with the ladies, as she was with other guys. We were young, and honestly, I didn't care. Not that I didn't care about her but that I realized the statistics of relationships that age lasting the long haul were slim. I can name one, but that's beside the point. Or maybe that is the point. But I didn't fuck every chick she accused me of. I did several of them, but not all. I never called her out on her strayings, indiscretions, or whatever you want to call it. Like I said, I was playing the statistical odds.

What started out as a hot and heavy relationship, based on wild romanticism, began turning stale. But we were, still are, stubborn. No one would admit things were declining between us or that things already had.

She wanted things to be steadier, not in an exclusive way. Yes, she wanted that, and to be honest, I did too. I think. Hell, I still don't know what I wanted. Maybe I just didn't want to lose her.

She wanted to know where things were going. She had plans for her future. She wanted me to fit into them. I wanted her to fit into my future. That became a point of contention. She didn't want to be a glorified groupie, her exact words. I didn't want a white picket fence in a suburb, working nine to five for a company that'd give me a gold watch after thirty years, causing me to recreate a Keanu/Bullock movie.

This was it, our inability, or unwillingness, to compromise—the cliched beginning of the end. Once this was out in the open, everything turned into a fight. From what movie to watch, to where to eat, to how often we were having sex. That last one though is a bit more legitimate of a point than the others. But nevertheless, everything was a fight.

We said we had both stopped seeing other people, which I did and she did too. I trusted her when she said that. But the damage was done. From the first part of our relationship being open, non-exclusive, free, polyamorous, whatever bullshit label of the moment you put to it, the feelings were there. And yes, the label was bullshit. No relationship stands the test of time when you're sticking your dick in other women and she's getting pounded by other guys. It doesn't work. Someone eventually wants more. Whether you call it intimacy, emotion, closeness, whatever. Someone, in some way, always wants more, and that doesn't come in a non-exclusive relationship. If I know anything, I've learned that in life, anyone who says differently about monogamy is, or will be, wrong. It didn't help any that we were both still friends with, and talking to, some of those people we previously bumped uglies with. And that led to suspicion and jealousy and mistrust: all three are not a basis for excellent relationships.

As I said, we were stubborn. The fights we had about who called, who we saw that night, why the other couldn't go with. As much as we both wanted *time apart with just our friends, the ones that were not mutual between the two of us, we didn't see it that way. Not when it came from the other person. We saw red. We saw everything that was in our minds. We saw the other person doing things that we may have done in the past with them happening now. And it snowballed. All because our perceived futures weren't as smoothly blended as Neapolitan ice cream. So neatly packaged and yet separate in the packaging.*

But it stayed like this till we graduated. Almost four years of ups and downs, four years of pushing and pulling: all because neither of us wanted to admit that after about the first year, it should have ended.

I think we were both holding onto something. Holding onto what could be. What we thought the other could be if only the other would change a little, not looking at who the other was. What the other really wanted. No. We held onto the idea of love and the notion of the changes the other could make so that our relationship would be a picture-perfect Norman Rockwell. But honestly, who wants to be with someone if so many little things need to change about them to make the relationship work? Who wants to be that person? The one who takes a happy, functional, moderately well-adjusted individual and tweaks so many things about them—gives them such a make-over—that the end product is so far off from where the person once was they are almost, if not wholly, unrecognizable.

As time went on, I think we held onto that. But my art was my work. I loved my art. I loved Faith. I didn't want to let go of her. I didn't want to admit that things went wrong so long ago. But things add up. They seem little at first, but they add up. And when you see the sum of what they've become, it ofttimes isn't pretty.

We were at some party. A graduation party, I believe. Not that the type of party matters but the devil's in the details, right? We were both there. We had arrived with each other but quickly went our separate ways once inside.

The party itself was lovely. Hors-d'oeuvres laid out. A large selection of mid to high-end wine and alcohol I probably should have abstained from. An enjoyable buffet of Chicago delicacies, like Vienna beef hot dogs, Italian beef, and Lou Malnati's pizza. I do remember those details. I had conversations with people about future plans: who had jobs lined up, where some people were moving to, what we thought the future held. But I got talking to some guy. Hell, if I remember his name, or even what he looked like. Jay, John, Jack, whatever. It's not important.

What is important is that we were talking about me. My plans. I was saying to him how I wanted to stay here but maybe head to New York. Chicago had a good music scene. But so did New York City, and Orlando, and Venice Beach. But here was home. Here was where my music was rooted. But on the other note, New York City had a good scene for rock, punk, and underground. What I didn't realize then was the sum of everything I was saying was about my goals. I hadn't put any thought into what Faith wanted. But that was our relationship, all about the individual. Her plans didn't put me into account. Not saying that what I did was deserved. Neither of us deserved it. But as

I talked, I didn't realize that somewhere in our conversation, Faith had crept up behind me.

To this day I still don't know why she didn't make her presence known, but she didn't. Hell, maybe she did and I was so wrapped up in the conversation I didn't notice. She could have been all, "Finn. Finn! Finn!!" and I was just too damned caught up in the sound of my own voice, laying out my future plans that she could have been screaming bloody murder and I would have been oblivious. Which would make me a huge asshole, but I was used to being called that by this point. Maybe she didn't make herself known to me at that moment because she was searching for a reason. Wanting to find her excuse to blow it all up, but she heard me say something. Something about my upcoming album and going on tour via the record company's dime. That was when she chimed in.

"News to me." Her words were simple, pointed, sharp.

I did the quick introduction. "Blah blah, this is Faith. Faith, this is blah blah."

"I was waiting for a good time," I excused.

"Well, now's a good time," she attacked.

Blah blah saw that this was not going to be a polite conversation and snuck off somewhere after the introduction.

"So, I got signed." I kept my reply short.

"You've been playing enough and promoting enough," she said, as if my work was just play. A hobby.

People think that. They look at music, acting, art in general as just play. Something to do when bored. Something fun to do that doesn't take real time or energy. Like this shit just happens. Like we don't pour

our hearts, souls, blood, sweat, and tears into every ounce of it, hoping, praying, screaming to the skies above that it one day might be almost possibly worth all the pain and torment we put ourselves through. "Playing enough and promoting enough." Fuck her. Getting signed is not as easy as a label exec being at a show, papers ready, and signing you because they like your sound. It is much more complicated than that.

"And they want me to tour. Not headline. Just opening or mid-act. But tour," I continued, hoping this would calm things.

We had our public fights and her side fist beating me in a desperate panic of name-calling, hoping to make some significant breakthrough in our relationship. But damn if I wanted to do this here.

"And where am I in all of this?" She questioned my upcoming tour as if it was centered around her.

The record company didn't exactly give a crap about what woman was involved in my life or whether or not I needed Mommy or Daddy to tag along. Hell, they wanted to make money off me, and I wanted to play and, hopefully, pad my pockets.

But that's where things escalated. What was a quaint, peaceful party with a few drunken shenanigans had turned into a shouting match between us. I don't remember all of the argument, but I do remember bits and pieces.

"You said you didn't want to be a glorified groupie." The sarcasm wasn't just dripping off my chin; it was spewing everywhere. Sarcastic was how most things were said between us. "So, I didn't tell you yet. It's not *like you want to be a part of that anyway. Don't you have a job lined up in fucking Michigan or somewhere?"*

"On Michigan Avenue, you dumbass! I have no plans on leaving this city!" The volume of her voice rose above all other conversations.

People were watching by this point. I remember because of how stupid I felt over the "dumbass" comment. I remember because of how it ended.

At this point, she was crying. She didn't care who saw. She didn't care about being vulnerable. She wanted out.

"Things could have been wonderful. Full of life and love. But you pushed. You always cared more about yourself and your dreams than mine. All you needed was just a little faith in me," she wept.

I was not a crier. I'm still not a crier. I stood there, watching her cry, not shedding a tear. Maybe I was an asshole. I know I looked like one. I guess I was. Asshole is as asshole does.

"Your dreams never compromised to mine. We never compromised, even in the beginning. We are two uncompromising people. That's what makes us ... us." I was oblivious to the beckoning end.

"Made," she whispered. One word. And the tense of that word represented everything she needed to say. One little word: Made. And the resonation of it was deafening. The points were sharp, and they shot through my heart.

I pleaded. "What are you talking about, 'made'? This'll pass just like all the others." I was desperate. I sounded desperate, and I knew it. I didn't care. I didn't want to lose her.

"No. No, it won't because no matter what we do, no matter how hard we try to pretend that things work or that they will work... they won't. They haven't. For a long time, if ever." Faith sounded beyond defeated.

"But they will. You have to believe me. You gotta have faith. In me." I turned the phrase on her. I was hoping it would make her realize we both played a part in this and that there was still hope. If only we had faith.

"Perhaps. One day. In the future, perhaps. But now, our time has passed," she cried.

"No, it hasn't," I continued to plead. "It's only passed if we give up."

"And I've given up. I'm done. We can't pretend to be something we're not, and it's time to move on," Faith finalized, turned, and walked away.

I stood, not knowing what to say. Nothing witty came to mind. Nothing charming popped into my head to convince her to stay. No quick phrase to cause her to turn her head and smile at me, all anger swept away by my smile. No thrown punches from her that say in all their rage that she still loves me. Nothing. I just stood and watched as she walked away. Thinking, shouting in my mind to the universe to get her to turn around. To look me in the eye one last time. To see that I still want to be the man she needs—the man I thought I should be. But she didn't. I felt the universe had abandoned me.

The universe had other plans—for both of us.

CHAPTER 6

Garden Of Eden

Whatever her reasons for choosing Coffee Shop of Horrors I don't know, but I'm excited, nervous, and uncertain. Not to mention I'm curious about this place. I'm not sure what her life had in store for her. I'm not sure about anything. But she said coffee, and I wasn't about to object.

My day has only just begun and I need to chillax, to do some deep breathing. Meditate on my current situation if you will. Clear my mind. Since I'm not good at yoga, I figure what better place to shake the anxiety away than the Orlando Garden of Eden. The big magical kingdom fully equipped with a castle at dead center. The mouse and his little Mouseketeers. The local news changed the landfall time of the approaching hurricane to later tonight, so I went. If it rained a little, I wouldn't melt.

After leaving our little get-together last night, I spent a good portion of the remaining evening writing a new body of lyrics. Not sure if the words are poetry alone or if they need music, but I wrote. Perhaps the essence of poetry crept back in because of my encounter with Faith last night. Maybe it was something that has been trying to claw its way out of me for some time. A chick pounding with its egg tooth, finally breaking through its shell. Perhaps it was all coincidence. Possibly I'm just full of shit, but I wrote. Not my best work admitted, but far from my worst. "Remnants" I call it.

> Across the horizon ashes and debris.
> The only remnants of what once was
> When once we're we.

> Ruins remain that once stood tall,
> But the path always pushes forward
> Making giants fall.

> Massive machines move mountains aside
> Tearing down what walls we have built
> Behind which we hide.

> A spark ignites, and forests burn
> But still, we keep on forward
> Life lesson learned.

> Smoke still lingers from fires now doused.
> Reminding me of happier days
> Before smiles turned shouts.

> Across the horizon ashes and debris
> The only remnants of what once was

GARDEN OF EDEN

When once we were we.

Maybe a waltz? Something sad and melancholy. With a touch of The Animals to give it a timeless feeling. Or just pass it off to Nick Cave and have him give it the life, emotion, and style that only he can. After all, he wrote an entire album called *Murder Ballads*, and that was after his song, "Loverman."

As my forest green Grand Am comes to rest in the theme park's overpriced parking spot, I look over and see it on my passenger seat. Right next to a small, old coffee stain from a few years back, a receipt. Not just any receipt, mind you. A receipt with a phone number: Viv's number. I hold the torn edges of the crumpled paper in my hands, staring at it for a moment, thinking back to last night. The ecstasy and the agony of it. I pull out my phone and dial her number, deliberating if hitting send is the best idea I've had since moving here or the stupidest. Sometimes there is a spark of genius in stupidity, seldom but rarely. I was hoping this was one of those times.

Send.

My heart starts pounding in my chest with such force it hurts, causing physical discomfort from the number of butterflies I am feeling. More than but-terflies. An intestinal churning that pulls and twists, making me want to taste my breakfast again. But I hold it in. Her voicemail saves me from having to deep clean my car later.

"Hey Viv, it's Finn. Wanted to say thank you for last night. Thought I'd see if you'd like to accompany me to the parks today or if you follow the two-day rule and I broke it. Perhaps another time though. 212-867-5309."

The pounding in my chest calms down, and I swallow what mix of food and bile has made its way into my throat.

I hit end on my phone and thoughts pour in. Why did I have such trouble calling this woman? Did I call her too soon? Does anyone still follow that two-day waiting rule? If there is a waiting rule, is it still only two days or has it increased, making me seriously break it? What is it about her that makes her different from the countless others? There was no difference in our meeting. No difference in the way we flirted or the conversation that led up to the wondrous activity that transpired behind the trees. Since I've learned the joys of my genitalia, I've done the song and dance countless times. Sometimes the song finished, while sometimes, like Billy Idol, I ended up dancing with myself. Throughout the years, the dance may have changed a bit, becoming slightly more sophisticated or complex, but it's still the same at the root of it all. So, what's different? Something I must ponder.

I walk through the magical kingdom, looking around at the facade. The buildings, the workers, the life that flows through each animatronic as they sing about tiki rooms and shit. I pull back the veil and notice what's beyond the facade. The mansion and all its ghosts, the exterior walls and how if anyone took more than two seconds to admire the craftsmanship, they could see that they were built with wall hangings you can buy at any pop-up Halloween shop. Yes, it gets the job done, and perhaps it's only here for temporary purposes, but I notice it nonetheless, and for a split second, I see the ever so slightly exposed underbelly of the beast. But damn it if this isn't one of my favorites. So I enter, wait through the intro, as most of his rides have, and sit upon the throne of a tilt-a-whirl car that glides me through these family-friendly ghosts.

Having not been on this ride since childhood, I remember it quite differently. Back then, it had an aura of mysticism and awe to it that made me buy what he was selling. Made me believe that these ghosts were real. Trapped in an eternal dance they must endure, never leaving their dancing partner, which made me hope for them back then that they were with the one they wanted, instead of having to settle on loving the one they're with.

Now, it's still just as good, but for a different reason. Now I see it for what it is—smoke and mirrors. Perfectly executed to make even the wizard behind the curtain believe in it all. It also houses a countless assortment of mixed quality haunted house props. Something I notice only because of my skepticism. It's both enchanting and somehow disheartening all at the same time. The memories of my childhood naïvete replaced with the jaded cynicism of adulthood.

Screw it. Speed metal for those lyrics. Or thrash metal. Something reminiscent of Slayer circa *Seasons in the Abyss*. Write the music fast and hard, so the juxtaposition of the words on top gives it an almost sarcastic, begrudging feel. Maybe throw in a bunch of processor effects, overdrive on the vocals, give it a disco tempo, and turn it into something Rob Zombie would admire.

Now, he's a performer that doesn't get the full credit he deserves. Yes, he gets a ton of credit but also a ton of slack. Very phenomenal in concert. I never thought I'd see such an outwardly brutal, metal guy line dance to such heavy music, but essentially that's what he does. And somehow this guy makes it work. Makes everyone, as savage as they think they are, want to be him. A line dancing, unapologetic vegan of badassness who makes some of the best music around. Also, great to dance to and have sex to. A master ability to equalize us all and help us forget our problems for a short while.

After my thoughts settle down, I find myself ho ho ho and a bottle of rum halfway through the pirates. Another ride perfectly executed. It calms me down, brings me back to a happy spot, which is nice because in just over an hour, I'm going to have to sit down with Faith and face my past. Why would I agree to this? Why would she propose such an idea? I don't know. Childish excitement over things long past? Maybe. A naïve notion that sometimes fairy tales do come true? Perhaps. Possibly I can act grown up enough to have her not walk out on me again. Maybe she'll see I am a real boy. By the time all these thoughts stop marathoning circles and finally settle down in my head, the faux British lady who guides my GPS has safely navigated me to the coffee shop.

Nestled in the corner of an unremarkable road next to a gas station and across from railroad tracks, it doesn't look like much. A small mom-and-pop coffee shop. I am not sure what to expect once I open the door, but the logo of a man-eating plant on the door lends a clue. The outside belies what is in. A giant LED TV plays *Puppetmaster*. Classic. The owner sits working on her laptop while casually watching the flick. Lamps for sale sit on numerous shelves, each individually made and hand-painted with skull bases. Very cool stuff. A giant hand-painted canvas with an artist rendition of Deadpool. Small paintings of original and artistic interpretations of horror themes decorate the rest of the walls: all also for sale. Two couches and two small tables fill the seating area. Then there's the coffee selection. The wall of blends is enough to make a coffee lover cry for joy. The shelves of flavored coffee don't lack variety either. Flavors like JudgeMint Day and V is for Vanilla Cinnamon and unflavored roasts like Burial Grounds and Shrieking Toad make this place feel like it may become one of my regular haunts, an adult's place of fantasy and caffeinated fun. That is if this meeting, date, whatever it is with Faith, goes well.

After looking around some more, I grab a cup of coffee and take a seat at a table. The couches are open, but I don't want to sit too close to Faith. Things may get uncomfortable, more so than last night. I only get to see about two minutes of the horror movie masterpiece before she walks in. She wears the same breathtakingly sexy outfit she wore my first night in Orlando. I'm not sure if she thought maybe I wouldn't recognize her if she wore something else or if it's just coincidence, but she is wearing it.

She smiles at me as she grabs her coffee. After putting in an inordinate amount of cream and sugar into a perfectly roasted coffee, to which the shop owner shakes her head and disappears into the back, she plops down on the couch I so strategically avoided.

"Much more comfortable." She gestures toward the couch.

I look at her waiting, wondering if I should sit there too or if this is where we are going to stage our long-awaited, possibly overdue, rendezvous.

"Come here." She pats the couch. "It's not like we're going to lose control of ourselves and go at it all hog-wild right here."

We laugh. It is nice, relaxing in a way that is also nerve-racking. She has a man. I should know her by now. Or at least know who she used to be. And that comment should be taken for what it is. A joke. Nothing more. So, I decide a seat on the couch isn't a bad idea after all. But I sit propped against the arm, a place I can lean against comfortably and make myself as far from her as I can, while still accepting her invitation to sit here.

Perhaps I don't know her at all anymore. Hell, she could have the clap or HIV. I don't know. How does she know I don't have either of those? She doesn't. Seventeen years is a long time.

"I like your outfit. Very Stepford goth chic." I figure a compliment is a good way to start things.

"Figured you would since the last time you saw me in it, you didn't even recognize me." A backhanded way to say thank you. Typical Faith. Some things never change.

It feels nice. New but familiar. An oxymoronic sentence if there ever was one. Like a new sequel to your favorite film: you know all the characters; you know the premise. Just excited to see how it all unfolds.

Time seems to stand still. The old laughter comes back, and it feels nice. Faith fills me in on her post-collegiate life. Her time spent in the business world, effectively being a white-collar woman in a corner office an elevator ride up each day and hating every minute of it. The corporate environment wasn't who she was after all. How repressed she felt. Suffocated. The enclosed elevator a daily reminder of her rat status in the race. She wanted a simple eyebrow ring, but office policy dictated otherwise. No piercings allowed except ears, no visible tattoos. (Which doesn't work well for someone who loves sleeveless tops.) But more than that, she says it was "the stifling of any and all original thought." The corporate brainwashing, the manifestation of the faceless kids from *The Wall* all grown up, carrying out the whims of their masters. No fighting back, no talking back. No resistance.

"I just woke up one day and asked myself, 'How did I get here? This isn't who I am.' I'm not sure it ever was." A big smile breaks out on her face. A smile that's so big it looks like it could hurt. "And I want to thank you for that. I think after all the ups and downs, you helped me get out of my shell. Discover who I was deep inside."

I've never had such kind words sting so strongly. I remain gracious and say nothing for a second, as my mind searches for the right words. Nothing about how she couldn't have realized this back then; we wouldn't be who we are now if she did. The story of us would not have ended the way it did. So, I say the only proper thing to say.

"Thank you. That means a lot." A forced smile comes out, but part of me still wants to run, kicking and screaming, throwing anything and everything I see. Some part of me wants to destroy something beautiful as a fuck you to the gods for ruining what could have been. My rebellion against the universe, but I just smile. I figure I'll turn this into some lyric set and music disaster piece later.

Time has a very peculiar way of opening old wounds at the worst possible moment. Possibly those are the only moments they can open up, as if the universe prevents the scab from being ripped off at the wrong moment. Planning and plotting to make sure the scar that forms has enough tissue to prevent any further injury. If only it would ever heal.

They don't heal. And as old wounds get scratched at like a bad mosquito bite, she has unknowingly scratched at mine.

As soon as I think she finishes, she takes one more strike at me. This time gouging away all formed scar tissue, plus an area around it, making sure that she got everything as if she were a doctor excising cancer. She tells me about him: the one-man wrecking crew of a boyfriend—Ronnie.

It's been nearly two decades since I've seen her. I should think this wouldn't hurt so bad, but it does. And it's her eyes. Those haunting eyes that make it hurt. If only they had not haunted my mind. Had her eyes not been the *Dream Police* living inside of my head, invading my sleeping mind, maybe hearing all this wouldn't feel as bad as it does.

But it does.

What is important to the point is this, I can't exactly get up and leave. I can't tell Faith to stop. The pathet-icness of either would be colossal. So, I listen as she recounts about how she met him at a concert. I hear her tell me about her vacation in New York half a decade ago. She had already been living in Orlando for a year and wanted to see the Big Apple. So, she went, a lone vacation to see what all the buzz was about. The bar in Queens she stopped at had the flyer for a local concert she saw promoting some up-and-coming bands. She was a fan of one of the musical groups and went. And that's where she ran into a guy also there on vacation from Orlando, a muscle-bound man hunk nicknamed Ronnie Frown.

The funny thing was, as she tells me about this show, the bands, the venue, something occurs to me. I helped set up this show. I helped get the bands lined up. I was helping promote some new punk trio that imploded on themselves in true punk fashion before they could explode onto the scene. But I helped put together the show that introduced my lost love to her current companion. I was the eagle shot with the arrow fashioned from my feathers. And the icing on the cake of this steaming pile of shit she is telling me is, "There was a part of me that was hoping to run into you while I was in New York."

Fuck me.

My mind shuts down; a protective measure to prevent permanent damage, I'm sure of it. Faith sits there talking and I hear the noise of her words, but I can't make them out. I see her lips moving, but I can't read lips that well. I am sure she knows I have faded from the conversation, but she keeps talking anyway because it would be rude of her to assume I'm doing something so bold.

Then she smiles, a smile I've never seen on her before. Or one she never had when she was with me. It looks happy.

"And that's why I asked you for coffee," she finishes.

Fuck me with a sideways dildo. *What did I miss? What did she say?* I can't ask. I can't admit that I spaced out because I am in grievous amounts of pain unintentionally caused by her. I'm not going to be that assface I was in the past.

"I was just surprised you asked me in the first place." I figure a neutral response would be fitting. Nothing that says I pretended to listen and hope this is what you want to hear. And nothing that can be so far off center that she walks out.

"It just threw me to see you that first night. At first, I thought you recognized me and weren't sure how to approach. But once I realized you didn't realize who I was, I thought I'd drop a subtle reminder for you to pick up." Her words just as I would have said them.

"I'm sorry about that. You just look so different."

"I know. More like someone you would have wanted back then."

That hurts. Deep. My stomach drops. I feel my heart slow. Is this the moment I pay the piper? I never was a crier, but I feel tears welling up in my eyes. But I hold them in. She doesn't mean for that to penetrate like it does. She is making a sarcastic comment about the state of tail I chased back then and how she outwardly appears now. But it shoots through my heart and clear through the other side because she is right.

She continues telling me that her current look has nothing to do with a deep-seated need to get me back or piss off her father. It has more to do with herself. Being who she is at the core of her soul, an outward expression of her innermost self. No arguments there.

I think it is at this moment I understand myself more than I ever have. All I have ever done is try to express that. In every song I write, in every chord I play, but it is just that. The pain flowing through me right now is also very relieving. Very soothing. I let the pain overtake my senses and heighten them. I feel more alive now, sitting in this wonderfully quaint Coffee Shop of Horrors, in more emotional pain than I've ever felt, as well as some manifested physical pain, than I ever have in all the sexual encounters, drugged-out states, or drunken nights long forgotten. I feel so alive because of her words. Both the pain and the joy they bring. The agony and the ecstasy.

She sees a change in my expression. She knows I want to say something that will be sentimental, something that can quite possibly ruin this moment. She grabs my hand.

"Don't get all pussified on me now. Whatever you are about to say, don't. I regret nothing. I wouldn't be who I am today without it all. I am very happy with that so far. And your dreams would never have come true if you sacrificed back then. So, don't say it. Just do what comes to you so unnaturally and force it down. Force yourself to keep it in."

Damn, she has grown. Changed. And it's the person she has become that seems so wonderful that even more now, I want to say something stupid enough to ruin the moment.

I smile a smile that says I'm happy and holding back tears of joy. The out-pushed lips and wrinkled nose. All my facial muscles are trying to reabsorb the salt water that has collected on my bottom eyelids. I swallow.

"It really is nice to see you again," I say, searching for words better suited for this moment.

"I'm glad," she says, pointing outside.

How did I miss it? Was the sound of the outdoors blended in with the soundtrack of the movie? Was I that enthralled with her? How did I miss the start of the storm? The lightning flashes in the not-too-far distance. The roaring clap of the following thunder. Hurricane Spiffy Giggle Bunnies, whatever the fuck it is named. *How the hell did I not notice? More importantly, how the hell is anyone going to drive in this crap?* The raindrops are the size of gumballs. Not the ridiculously big gumballs that crack your jawbone if you bite down on a stale one but the small gumballs. The orange-flavored ones that come in the mesh sack to make them look like Florida oranges. The darkening sky overhead says this storm is going to be anything but a party. Already the winds have picked up and are threatening to topple over anything not anchored down. Those meteorologists sure as shit screwed the pooch when timing this one out.

The owner emerges from the back, and much to her surprise, we are still there. We all lock eyes for that awkward moment you know is coming in a situation like this.

"Didn't think you two would still be here," she admits.

"Lost track of time. Apologies," I offer. But still, she must deliver the inevitable.

"We're closing up early. I hate to do this to you with the conditions, but..." she trails off.

"No worries." I alleviate her guilt.

I look at Faith and she looks at me, half smiling. Still getting a feel for the full layout of the greater Orlando area, I don't have much usefulness to add at this moment. She just stares as if she is waiting for me to say something. So, I stare back deeper into her eyes, hoping to uncover what she wants from me. Her smile widens from a half-cocked smile to a full-blown, brilliant idea, lighting up her mind smile.

"What?" is all I say, not sure where her thoughts are leading her and because of that, I'm not sure what else to say.

I find it interesting that for someone who writes as many lyrics as I do, I'm at a loss for words an awful lot of the time.

She laughs a half-forced, quiet laugh, then jumps up off the couch, smacking my thigh as she does. "Come on."

"Where're we going?" I ask, thinking about the fact that in like three seconds, I'll be outside in a torrent of hurricane winds and rain, being possibly smacked across the face by Anoles caught up in the wind. I'd like to know what I'm stepping out into that for.

"Don't you trust me anymore?" she asks.

Nice retort, but do I trust Faith? I haven't seen her in almost twenty years. We have had a pleasant conversation so far, and even the parts of the past brought back up didn't seem to deter any forward motion. So, as she stands before me, hand outstretched and staring down at me, I ask myself, *Do I trust her? Now, after all this time, do I have a legitimate reason not to believe her?*

Sure. Why not? What could possibly go wrong?

CHAPTER 7

My Heart, Your Hands

I am not sure what to expect. I don't think Faith is going to lead me to a forest, tie me up, and kill me. Though, the falling rain aside, the freshly dampened woods, and being tied up might make for a fun time. I think that maybe she knows a place close by that will be open. Possibly a friend's house for a hurricane party. As I said, I am not sure what to expect.

I drive, following behind her through the hurricane, King and Foxtail palms swaying in the wind and rain. My mind is continually trying to focus on the barely visible road and not die, but at the same time, all I can think about is where she might be taking me. The possibilities are endless. Each raindrop that tries shattering my windshield is a momentary torment teasing me about the fragility of this life. They are also incomprehensibly shouting at me the innumerable places yet to see in The City Beautiful. We stop in the parking lot of an apartment complex. Each building identical to the next in color and height: tan with terra-cotta, Spanish tile roofing. I don't recognize this place. Though what little I can make out through the torrent of water gushing down from the skies above, I see no neon signs. No restaurants beckon for business. The rain still pounds down on our cars, but at least we are not moving. It strikes down in full force and gives my mind a new place she might take me. The drive was maddening, and we both somehow survived.

I sit in my car, engine running, trying to re-oxy-genate my body after an hour of what was apparently me holding my breath. I quickly flip down the sun visor to check myself in the mirror. My pale face slowly regains color as the terrified expression that had taken control gradually relinquishes power. I'm alive. And here I sit, parked next to her in this lot.

I see her exit her car and wave me to follow. So, I do. I get out and, in about point two seconds, am drenched head to toe, again. I was halfway dry after the dash out of the coffee shop. But it's cool. I figure we are going to a hurricane party at Ronnie's or something.

Up a flight of covered stairs that should provide cover from the storm except that the wind is blowing the rain almost entirely horizontal, Faith stops at a door labeled 217. From outside the windows, there appear to be no lights on. At least not enough illumina-tion to warrant a hurricane party. I can't hear much as the rain relentlessly assaults my ears to a deafening point. Faith pulls out an unremarkable gold key and opens the door.

Hung, framed pictures of her family and friends decorate the walls. A dirty ashtray beside a half-smoked pack of reds, topped with a green, plastic lighter, sits on her relic of a coffee table left over from the early nineties, complete with a black porcelain cat base that holds the glass tabletop. But the smell of the stale cigarette smoke takes my mind back to our happier times. The days of wine and roses, so to speak. Days when she would sit beside me as I wrote songs on the guitar, drinking whiskey, and smoking cigarette after cigarette.

She shakes out her long, pitch-black curls, whipping me back to the present tense where her hair is no longer straight and dirty blonde. She asks if I would like some bourbon, but the tone of her voice tries to mask the true intention of her words. My only thought is a throwback to the TV show *Friends*. "Does Joey want two pizzas?" I smile as I fruitlessly squeegee myself off in her doorway. As the water drips from my body, so does the weight holding back my words.

"Booker's, if you have some."

Faith grabs two cordial glasses from her cabinet and some ice from the fridge. For herself. Then as she holds my glass up to the ice dispenser, she tosses me a silent question.

"Neat, please."

She refrains from assaulting the glass with ice and fills it in bourbon. Beautiful, oaky bourbon.

She hands me the glass while looking me up and down. She sets her glass down on an end table littered with unopened mail, conveniently located both right next to the door and the couch.

"You're soaked. Let me put your clothes in the dryer." Faith starts undressing right in front of me.

"Um, what?" I say, completely caught off guard. All I can think is that this is not the same woman from Coffee Shop of Horrors, telling me, "It's not like we're gonna jump each other right here." Or whatever she actually said. This isn't even the gal from our first night of margaritas and definitely not the lady who walked away at the end. But then again, we weren't at the coffeehouse, and she was way past any other moment we shared.

By the time my thoughts die down, she is in her bra and panties. She's wearing next to nothing and still wears it as well as she did back then, if not better.

"Come on, cowboy. Not like it's nothing we haven't seen before," she says, solidifying her case.

"Okaaayyy," I say, a bit off guard.

But still, I undress down to my boxers and give her my wet clothes. She walks only a few feet down a short hall and opens a set of louvered bi-fold doors to her laundry machine. She tosses them in the dryer and grabs a couple of bath towels so we can finish wiping ourselves off.

As I pat myself down, I watch as the towel slides across her damp skin, soaking up the moisture in its path. The towel climbs her leg that I wish was begging for me to kiss it. The curls in her hair try to re-stake their claim from the water. Her hips used to call out to me to be kissed, to be held. Perchance tonight. The towel glides up and past her chest. A chest topped with two of the loveliest breasts a person could wish for, perfectly shaped and sized to match her figure. At this moment, my mind cries out to every inch of flesh that stands in front of me and shouts to the past to reenact every position that ever was. But alas, that is only in my mind.

She proceeds to turn on some Static-X. Wonderful, techno-thrash. The funny thing is, this album is such a far cry from their other works before it. But, at the same time, it could never have happened if it wasn't for the previous albums. It is the perfect blend of everything before and yet a unique monster unto itself.

We sit on her couch in nothing but towels, drinking wonderfully aged bourbon. I do wonder what warrants her accommodating my request for such an elegant spirit. At least my cellphone is next to me, karmically saving me if and when I need. Hopefully.

There's an awkward silence. We both sit, mostly naked, sipping our bourbon. Faith on one end of the couch and I on the other with the middle of the sofa the barrier between us. Her eyes look me over, examining twenty years of change. The left corner of my lip turns up. I feel myself smiling both awkwardly and happily. My eyes turn toward the ceiling. I know I'm making this more uncomfortable than it is. I don't want her to think I am here just for a wham-bam-thank-you-ma'am. Yes, I want to have fast, explosive sex so intense it induces an aneurysm. Anyone attracted to the female form would desire the same. Some have even been so bold as to say they ain't too proud to beg if need be. But it's not my intention. So, I look toward the ceiling in all its flat, off-white glory. I hear a small, dismissive laugh. I sit unsure of what to say or do next, as if time has looped and this is our first night together.

Both ready to explore new lands, uncertain of the other's willingness and, at the same time, afraid of what the expedition might have in store.

My hesitant eyes turn back to her. A dubious answer to her chuckle. We both quietly stare into each other's eyes. Not searching for their soul. Not even looking for answers to the moment's unanswered questions. Just silently waiting for them to make a move. Whoever moves first loses the fight of the wills. So, I sit. I want so badly to say something to her: to tell her she still has the body of a goddess, to tell her that looking at her in her towel that has all but fallen off has me half-chubbed, to tell her that this night is so unclear in my mind as to what it means that I'm paralyzed, not with fear, but by the unknown. I start to say something, but it is really just noise. Something a toddler would gargle with uncoordinated vocal cords. So, I stop it quickly and finish the solid three shots of bourbon left in my glass.

She grabs my glass and heads back into the kitchenette. "Ronnie's a nice guy." She pours me another glass of bourbon. "And he loves me. But it's just ... sooo boring. There's no excitement. No surprises. The thrill is gone."

Choice words to shatter the silence.

I think the moments proceeding her words prove Depeche Mode wrong. There was nothing to enjoy in the silence.

"And I'm your excitement for the evening. A sort of take-home entertainment?" I say half- playful, half-seriously, inquiring if this is leading somewhere.

"I didn't think you'd mind." Honesty pours forth from her as she sits back down—this time a little closer to me.

"I don't ... but what about Ronnie?" I inch closer to her.

"Didn't I just cover that?" Always the quick wit. She leans in toward me. Not close enough to touch, but I can smell what perfume is left from the rain.

"I don't mean that. I mean the guy's literally twice my size. He could kill me without a struggle." I lean in closer to her.

She laughs, backing off a bit. "He's not going to find out."

"Unless he comes home."

"He's stuck at work till God knows when." She stands up and drops her towel. Her still drying bra reveals her gorgeous dark pink nipples. She turns and slowly struts her way to, I assume, her bedroom. Her panties tease me as she walks away.

I stand and take my first step toward re-entering a world I've long been estranged. My phone lights up. A number not yet programmed into my phone but recognizable all the same: Viv. The universe hates me, or it's trying to save me. I've done many, many, many, many things in my time that I am sure I need to pay for if I haven't already. But here I am. The one that made me who I am today, half-naked and ready to go on one hand. On the other hand, calling me is the new girl I can't get out of my mind, who is amazing in her own right. A devil on one shoulder and a seemingly less mischievous devil on the other. Whatever I may have still owed the universe, whatever karma there was left to pay back, this conundrum cleans my slate.

I pause. My head shifting between the phone and the woman down the hall, the phone cosmically beckoning me while Faith literally beckons me. This is the moment I've been waiting on for close to twenty years. I let the call go to voicemail and take a hopping step toward her room.

I turn into her doorway as she lights a candle. Three others already lit. It makes me wonder how long I was staring at the phone, but they are lit. She holds a joint between her lips as the smoke encircles her face. A moving frame. The universe whispering, "This is the choice you should have made tonight." I'm glad I did. She takes a hit and hands it my way. I inhale a short sample of the wares. I stop to get a feel for the product. I find it worthy. I inhale more. Deeply. Not only to take in the smoke but to inhale this event, take it in for all I can. The color of the deep red, softly scented cinnamon and sugar candles, the dark blue color of her matching set of bra and panties. Static-X's "Invincible" playing in the background, perfectly timed for this moment. I savor it for all the fleeting moments it provides, for this may never happen again. And even if it does, it will never happen like this again. Never like this. This is a unique, once-in-a-lifetime chance to change everything.

So, I will.

I exhale. My mind has captured all it can. And all it will. The THC starts doing its subtle job on my mind, relaxing me to a state I am far more comfortable with. Much more familiar with over the passing years. I try not to but accept the fact that a boyish grin has taken over my face. I let it happen as my smile raises my left eyebrow and lowers my right. Silently saying, "Yes! Yes, I can smell what The Rock is cookin'!" And it is glorious.

She points her finger at me with her upturned hand and motions me to her. As the Rock did when he entered the ring, I too will dominate. Or be dominated. Whichever. Tonight, I don't mind.

I drop my towel. My soldier is standing at attention. We both stop for a moment out of renewed admiration for what we see—out of the fact we just smoked some fantastic shit—and, well, because we're both comfortably numb.

She looks me up and down, biting her bottom lip as she unclasps her bra. As her lacey bra slips down past her nipples, Victoria reveals her best-kept secret. Oh, how I've missed those. They say you can never go home again. Damn those fuckers. Damn those fuckers to hell. Daddy's home. And I am happy to be here again.

I step to her as she moves onto the bed. She turns on her back, looking at me, smiling. I find I still fit so perfectly between her legs as they wrap around me. She pulls me in close, kissing me as we hover somewhere between sitting up and lying down. I return her kiss with gusto. A kiss I've thought about for years, lips whose touch I've missed. A woman whom most of my songs were about. A moment. This moment. This singular moment that's been ingrained in song over and over, manifesting in my THC and alcohol-fueled mind. And it feels better than I have ever imagined. Every song that I wrote about this moment. Every chord ever strummed in an ode to this moment all pale by comparison. Those weren't the greatest. No. They were just a tribute. You gotta believe me.

She playfully bites down on my lower lip, pulling me down onto the bed. I put out my arms so as not to fall on top of her, but I misjudged my distance. Her teeth scrape my lower lips, drawing a drop of blood as she releases. I don't flinch. Don't say a word. Just lick the inside of my lip, taste the crimson, and smile. Lowering my head to wrap my lips around those nipples that have been so longing for my touch.

As the Static-X album comes to an end and our quiet moans of consent are all that fill the otherwise silent air, Tenacious D's "Fuck Her Gently" comes to mind. I am going to take this as a cosmic sign of what I should be doing. Because, to paraphrase the song, sometimes you must fuck gently. Then fuck hard. And as if the universe gave her the same message, without the pomp and circumstance that is the dance we call foreplay, she slides me inside her. Deep.

"Fuckin' metal!" The words slip out of my lips. Verbal diarrhea to kill the mood. A phrase I haven't uttered in a long time, a phrase I've never used to describe sex. She looks quizzically at me. A first in a long, many years. A smile breaks out on her face as she begins to laugh.

"Fuckin' A, it's metal!" a perfect reply.

This is going to be fun.

So, I follow the lead of Tenacious D. I lean in. I kiss her chin and make my way down her neck. She quivers a bit. I begin to slide my hand up her stomach as I kiss my way down. I feel every inch of me slowly slide in and out of her. Her breathing deep and intense. I slide my other hand behind her arching back. I feel the seventeen years of unspoken love, or some feeling perceived to be love, spilling out at this moment.

She leans in, nibbling on my ear. Then a commanding whisper. "Hard and fast, loverboy. Don't puss out on me now." A demand I did not expect, nor one that I will ignore. Sorry, Mr. Black; tonight, there will be no gentle fucking. Only hard, fast, dirty, and fun.

And at that moment, I hear the guitar riff. Unmistakable in its sound. Simple yet always drawing in the listener for more. The opening riff that embraced what the eighties were all about. "Talk Dirty to Me."

So, I begin to speed up, finding how hard and fast she wants it. My man is in no mood to finish anytime soon. We have as long as we need.

The headboard begs for mercy with each smack against the wall. The frame starts squeaking more and more with each pump of my piston into her well-oiled, overflowing engine. The deluge of juices flowing from her is something new to me. Not that I've never had a lady gush or squirt on me, just not her. Faith was not that woman before. This is a welcome change. I, like many of my brethren, can appreciate the puddle, the squirt, and all of its sprinkler, water park-like qualities.

We explore the changed landscape of our bodies. Seeing what is new and what we have missed over the years. Soaking in the pool of sweat and juices dripping off our bodies. Faith's painted claws scratch down my back, over and over, digging into me. Deeper and deeper. Leaving their marks, claiming me for her.

The floorboards joining in the chorus of plaintiff cries for mercy the headboard first started. The speed increasing exponentially. First a fast-paced sports car. Now a jack rabbit after ten lines of coke and a bottle of NoDoz. All at her moaning behest. As she tenses her kegel muscles, only a few p.s.i. from separating the manhood from the man, she stops me. Pulls me down next to her and whispers into my ear the three little words, the holy grail, the most elusive phrase that every man secretly wants to hear but that after all these years, I never expected to pass my ears.

"Fuck my ass."

Generally not a first date activity, but then again this wasn't our first date. I pause for a brief moment out of shock. The audacity that someone who hasn't known me in years would assume that such a request would be met. But then again the look in her eye shakes me free. I am not one to deny this request from such a beauty of a woman. I flip her around and get a view of her heavenly, heart-shaped ass. If I weren't a participant at this moment, it would bring a tear to my eye that such a smooth, perfectly shaped ass exists. With tan lines in the perfect spot to exemplify the heart shaped-ness of it all.

I give it a nice, hard smack for good measure. Faith cries out in pleasure, "Yes! Daddy!" Also, a phrase we never explored back then. A most welcome addition.

I spank her again and grab her hair. A handlebar, if you will, to steady my way in. With all the wetness provided from tonight's activity, entering her presents no challenge. She has done much self-discovery in the years between. I'm enjoying the spoils of her explorations.

"Yes!"

"Yes!!"

"YES!!!"

I spank her again as I thrust harder, deeper, faster. The slapping of skin against skin has never sounded so good. This is the moment the midnight hour was made for.

"I want you to cum," she cries out.

"You'd better not cum in her, asshole!" Ronnie yells out.

We must've missed the sound of him coming in. The turn of the handle, the slam of the door, drowned out by the sounds of hurricanes and sex.

I pull out, fearing for my safety as the behemoth of a man charges toward me. But it's too late. Bodily functions quickened by the emotional yearning for the climax can only be put off so long. I may be out, exposed for all my glory, but my guy has something to say. Ronnie sees me spitting on his floor my batch of Wite-out and stops in his tracks. I juke passed him, out of the bedroom. I reach into the dryer for my clothes while sprinting down the hall with a full erection, but all I manage to grab is a sock. No pants, no wallet, no keys. Just one sock.

I can't make another pass at the dryer. The only exits out of the apartment are the door I entered through and the balcony with its two-floor descent, both of which are on this side of the hallway.

I run into the makeshift dining room and bunker behind the dinner table. Ronnie runs into the living room and stops upon seeing me. His chest heaves up and down. Veins on his arms bulge out, ready to explode in a torrent of pain all over my face. His mind calculates the countless ways he can tear each limb from my body in the most painful way possible.

"Calm down now, big guy!"

I say the first thing that comes to mind, but not what Ronnie wanted to hear. He circles around the table as I round the other direction. A newly started game of cat and mouse, but he stops where I just stood.

His silent intimidation breaks. "Calm down?! Calm down?! You just had your dick in my woman's ass! Then came all over my fucking bedroom and you want me to calm down!? I'll fucking kill you, you piece of shit!"

He jumps onto and over the dining room table, hurtling toward me.

Faith, still in her birthday suit, bolts into the living room and gets in his path.

"Ronnie! Stop!" she pleads.

He stops. Looking at her, his face turns a darker shade of red, as a vein in his forehead bulges out so much I may be saved by an aneurysm.

"I'm not even close to stopping." He shoves her out of the way.

A gesture that I do not take kindly to, I forget the size difference for a split second.

"Hey! That's not very gentlemanly of you, bro," I say, stepping toward him. Like I can actually do anything to intimidate this Goliath.

"Gentlemanly?"

He lets out a chuckle. Maybe I was wrong. Perhaps he possesses the ability to reason and things will turn around.

"Fuck you! Bro!" His fist connects with my head. The sound of which echoes through my ears. A thud rings through the apartment as the sudden stop of my head and torso against the floor pulls all the air out of my lungs.

Or reasoning is beyond him.

I'm stunned. I know I'm dazed but my brain, much like Ronnie at this moment, says, "Fuck you" to me. I can't move. I see him towering over me. All three hundred pounds of attack, but I can't move. I can't run. At least for this moment. I am stuck. He looks down, shaking his head at the patheticness that is me right now. He spits on me as he turns his head back to Faith.

Right in my face. I guess in some way I deserve this. I knew this night was too good to last, too perfect to end well. But at least my senses have returned to me. So, I stand and wipe the spit and pride off my face. And while I don't appreciate the spit on my face, I'm confident he's not going to cut out the pieces of carpet or sheets with my semen on it and have them framed. I'm doubly convinced he's not thrilled about my sperm on his girlfriend.

"So, are we even now?" I hope to calm the situation.

He turns back to me after he and Faith finish some inaudible exchange that I'm certain was not loving. He looks into my bruising face, swings again, and hits the other side.

Once again, I find myself kissing the carpet. But at least this time I can get back up.

"Get out." He sidesteps a direct answer.

"Can I least get my clothes?"

"Can I hit you again?" He opens the door.

While the thought of my clothes is a nice one, it is much outweighed by the pain induced by his massive sledgehammer of a fist. I stand naked for a second and look at Faith. She mouths to me words that usually end a date with no further contact. "I'll-Call-You."

Ronnie turns back to see what she's saying, a moment I seize to grab my phone and run.

The door shuts behind me, leaving me standing in the hallway of an apartment complex.

Naked.

Wet.

With one sock.

And a phone.

I take the sock and cover my cock. A cocksock if you will. It's better than nothing. Not that anyone is out in this storm this late at night. The floor above me provides little shelter from the raging storm. But enough to use my phone.

I dial D.B., but he does not answer. Voicemail, a savior, does not make. As the rain beats down on my naked body, I know I must do something fast before someone sees me, before the cops are called, before this escalates worse than it already has. Peering down at the clock reading 12:30 on my phone, I can think of only one person. One person who will answer my call, because she is waiting for me to return her call—hoping for me to call. There is this voice in the back of my mind telling me not to call. Not now. Not when nothing I can say to her about this will paint me in a good light. Another voice chimes in. It reminds me that I shouldn't care, that I owe her nothing. One good conversation and a blowjob is not the foundation for a monogamous relationship. For all I know, she could be in bed being railed by some guy right now. It's not my business. Though I do find that thought a little less appealing than I'd like.

The rain is a little cold. And it's not doing my guy any justice. It looks less like those old children's toys that slipped out of your hand the more you tried to hold onto it and more like a scared turtle hiding in his shell. Just the icing on the cake that is this hurricane.

So, I find a place to lay low. I duck behind these valet garbage bins that seemingly double as benches and find shelter for my body. No need to alarm any busybodies that inevitably peek out the windows, checking to make sure no burglar is taking advantage of the rain to commit robberies.

I dial.

Before my mind begins to doubt my latest action, I hear it ring. I can't hang up now. That will just look weird. It rings again. I can only hope that her voicemail picks up. It rings a third time. Voicemail may make a savior yet. Fourth ring. If she hasn't picked up by now, she won't.

"Hello?"

Damn. Here's hoping.

CHAPTER 8

Down In It

*T*he events of the day got me thinking about New York, why I loved it and why I needed to leave it. I wonder if my actions here are nothing more than a new way to repeat the same mistakes. I wait naked in the rain, thinking about my last fling in the Big Apple.

I remember looking around the stranger's room I was lying in. The abstract artwork reminiscent of, but not quite, a Rothko stood out like a sore thumb against the beige walls. The iPod dock in the background played some rock radio station. The thirty-five-inch LED screen waited to be clicked to life. It was nice but ordinary. A female voice on the radio started talking about Florida. Something in the smoky, yet nurturing tone of the lady's voice struck a memory I once held close but had been a little lost as of late. Something once said to me, "Never do anything you wouldn't tell your parents about."

I have about twenty years of memories I would never tell my parents about. Nights of love and lust, topped with the smooth creaminess of more desire and more moments lost to the demon known as alcohol, when all you wanted to do is hold onto the memory of what was happening right then. Days when a good bag of weed could take away all the worries of the next tour, the next song to be written, the album cover to design, but instead of a much needed bag of weed, you find yourself talking down three gunmen in a Truxican standoff all over some misunderstanding that probably wouldn't have happened if they weren't high in the first place. And while I guess what someone tells their mother or father depends on the type of rela-tionship they have, the premise still stands. Nights like that are not what a parental figure wants to hear about. No mother or father wants to hear about the latest romper room activity of their adult child or the name of the one-night stand lying in bed next to them.

But I make no apologies about who I am. I'm not a horrible person. I'm not down with the needle or the torched spoon. I don't raise my fist to the ladies. I don't needlessly berate people for some sick enjoy-ment. I'm a person who is playing the hand life dealt, and while I may have played into that hand, I am doing the best that I can because life doesn't let you go back and change the past.

I stretched, arms above my head, elbows bent in a full body stretch I felt in my toes. As I rubbed the sex out of my eyes, a thought entered my mind. I didn't know her name, the one-night stand that was next to me. I didn't know her name. I smiled a smile on my face that became more weathered each year, a smile that she'd think is real. It was real, to a point. But only in so much as to let the inner Hustler magazine-reading teenager in me have his moment. The blue satin sheets on her bed strewn about, tangled, and intertwined in a way that only a sweaty, heart-pounding, roll in the sheets can do. I finished my stretch and turned to her to see her staring at me: Finn Fairlane, Producer-Extraordinaire.

Who the hell cares? That's right. Her. It's why she continued talking to me barside at Sunswick once she realized who I was. I needed some strange, and here she was: a beautiful stranger with hazel-brown eyes, a mile-wide smile, and cosmetically enhanced breasts that were on full display. This is how I get inspired. The sexcapades that help me write, help me get direction to songs that have yet to be written. No, I'm not going to say they're getting old, or that they're losing their value for inspiration. They just haven't been doing it for me. There's been nothing in them to take away from. Like a Michael Bay flick, they are fun and full of adventure and excitement, but when the movie is over, there's not much to say about it except it was fun. All I could do at that moment was listen to the radio in the background finish the commercial about Florida vacations and how incredible they are. I thought maybe they are incredible. I didn't know. As an adult, I'd never been. But why the hell was I thinking about Florida when I had a naked woman lying next to me?

"You doin' okay?" She asked as she smiled at me. She fell back on the pillow, her blonde hair in need of *a root touch-up, either that or ombre hair, billowing out as if she was in a shampoo commercial.*

That's a loaded question: I was not doing okay. If I were, I wouldn't have been thinking about the radio commercial. I'd have been thinking about the naked lady next to me. But that wasn't an answer she wanted to hear.

"Dandy." I turn to get out of bed.

She laughed a little, coy laugh. "Dandy. I like that."

I could have said "Super Duper" in my best Peter Boyle a la Young Frankenstein or even done a damn air guitar while saying "Excellent" and she would've responded the same. She was just hoping I'd listen to her Bandcamp or ReverbNation page and make her and her band the next big thing. I wouldn't have landed her otherwise.

There I went giving her the same line I've given a hundred times to others: "I thought you would."

"Last night wasn't about anything," she started.

I looked at her curiously as I pulled up my dark wash denim jeans. "What did you think I thought it was about?" I asked.

"Didn't want you to think I was only sleeping with you..." She trailed off for a moment. Her head tilted as I waited for her to finish her thought, jean button in my hand paused for her. "Cat Claw. I didn't want you to think it was about my band or anything."

I finished buttoning up my jeans and reached down for my shirt. I knew she was waiting for some sort of affirmative response that fooled me into thinking that she was honest. But one, an upfront person wouldn't feel the need to make the statement. And two, if it really had nothing to do with her wanting me to help her band, then why not-so-subtly drop the name in there? And three. Cat Claw? Worst. Band name. Ever.

I took my time pulling my shirt over my head. "Of course not. Why would I?"

The look of both confusion and relief that mixed on her face was funny. It made her look both beautiful and ugly at the same time. "Oh. Okay. Just making sure."

"We're good. But I have to go meet a client."

"At this hour?" She slinked toward me a little in a meager attempt to get me to stay.

I huffed a small laugh. "It's early tomorrow morning. I need to actually get some sleep."

Her eyes widened with hope. "Can I call you?"

I felt my face start to grimace. I stopped it in the hope that I caught it early enough so she didn't notice.

"I don't give out my number. Too many unsavory individuals who present fine enough at first."

She nodded an almost imperceivable nod of understanding and disappointment that somehow a one-night stand didn't make the cut. I looked around and grabbed a torn-open envelope and a pen that was next to it.

I handed them to her, and she jotted down her number. I hugged her, giving the obligatory, "I'll call you." The funny thing though was as I hugged her, I thought that maybe I should listen to her band. Possibly I should call her again. I wasn't thinking that she was going to turn into something more than that: consensual sex between two consenting adults with no commitment to each other. But she did take the time out of her evening to give me some strange. But then, that was the same pattern of thoughts I had every time someone wanted me to do something for them and preempted the hopeful favor with sex.

As I walked down the hall to the cramped elevator in that Brooklyn building, a thought stirred in my mind: a sense of déjà vu. I got an eerie feeling about that hall. Maybe not that hallway in particular but that building. I didn't notice it on the way to her place, possibly because she had her legs wrapped around me while directing me as my eyes were staring at her chest. I wasn't really taking in my surroundings. But on my way out, free of distractions, free of blood being taken from my brain to fuel other body parts, I realized I had been there before.

The elevator buzzed and the door opened. A well-built man stood in front of me. Lean and muscular with a tight, maintained haircut. Chiseled jaw and tan skin. A Godsmack sun logo tattooed on his left arm. A gray tank-top and black workout pants. He looked at me with a slight head tilt. He grinned a slight gap-toothed grin. It hit me—why I recognized this hall—why that guy was maniacally smiling at me: Patrick.

I dashed toward the stairwell door, his words echoing in my head. "I thought I told you never to come back here, you piece of shit, Fairlane!"

I swung the metal door open and frantically started down the concrete stairs in dire need of a new paint job.

"I wasn't with her tonight!" I yelled back, hoping he would have stopped pursuit.

But I heard him enter the stairwell and a memory came to my mind clear as day. Another reason my time in NYC was up. It was this same stairwell; me *running down the same stairs while a woman, confused about her life choices, pleaded with her boyfriend to not bash my head in. I did appreciate that. The other part of that memory was the bat swinging down at my hand on the railing, narrowly missing. Had he connected, it would have certainly shattered my bones into a thousand pieces. The bat denting the banister itself, which I found out because my hand ran over the indentation from the last escape attempt.*

He was gaining ground. His aerodynamic body added to his physical advantage. I had to take half a staircase at a time. I prayed I didn't miss and sprain an ankle. I really didn't want a sprained ankle to be the reason my life ended that night.

His scream echoed in the stairwell as an audible exclamation, "You're dead meat!"

I don't think even Kiefer Sutherland could have made it sound any more threatening. I leapt onto the second floor. Adrenaline pumped hard through my heart, and so I did something I would never have done under normal circumstances. I jumped all the steps going from the second to the first floor. I somehow, by the grace of God, landed perfectly. No sprained ankle or broken bones.

As I opened the door to the lobby to make my getaway, Patrick attempted the same jump I had just landed. He was not quite so lucky. Both his ankles gave out under him, which caused him to fall forward, face first into the edge of the door. A loud smack of bone against metal caused crimson to splash out from his nose. A second crack echoed as he hit the concrete floor.

"Lucky bastard" slurred from his bloody lips as he looked up at me.

"I wasn't with her. I did heed your warning last time. I didn't know where I was till I was leaving."

I stood a few feet from him, unsure of what he may do as that scene played out in the lobby of the building. The door opened behind me and Patrick laughed. *"You weren't lying. Hi, Katy."*

I turned to see her standing there. The reason I ran down five flights of stairs in record time. The reason Patrick was bleeding and most likely broken on the ground. At 5'2" and maybe a buck twenty as she shakes off the rain. Waist long, straight dark brown hair. Pouty lips on an innocent face. Katy.

She looked down at him. *"What happened?"*

"Nothing, babe."

She turned to me for confirmation. *"Nice to see you again, Finn. Did this have anything to do with you?"* she said, as she grabbed an inordinate amount of facial tissue out of her purse.

"Misunderstanding. Let's help him up. He's too injured."

Patrick applied the tissue to his bleeding nose, then looked at me confused. Why did I help him after not once but twice he had threatened my life? Because the circumstances we find ourselves in in life are ofttimes beyond our control. When confusion reigns and people become reactionary, the ones who are granted forethought are not allowed the ability to forego civility. So, I helped him.

We each helped carry him like a beaten champ away from a fight. Little did he know that battle was with himself.

"Nice to see you again, Katy. This guy seems to be very protective of you."

"Yes, yes he is. And it's much appreciated. So, what are you doing here?"

I looked at him as he ever so slightly shook his head once. I, in return, gave an almost unperceivable nod.

"I was leaving, actually. After I help you to the elevator, I think Patrick can handle himself from here."

I pushed the elevator call button and turned to them both. I saluted them, two fingers to my forehead. "It's been a gas."

Headed to the main door, I turned back around as I heard them enter the elevator. "Katy, take care of each other."

She smiled before they disappeared behind the closing door.

I started walking down the street. Each step covered me a little more in the rain. As I hailed a cab, something made me think. I'd been in New York the better part of two decades. I loved that city. The overcrowded cemeteries that are hauntingly beautiful were always a thought on my mind. They stay with you. The end shot of Gangs Of New York does a perfect job of showing the monster that is this city. How lives that were once so important at one time are lost to the ever-growing entity that is NYC. But they do; they stick with you. However, at that moment, it wasn't the cemeteries. It was the fact that there are innumerable buildings in the boroughs with even more countless rooms within. And I had found a way to start going through them again. It stabbed me right below my ribs, pain that I shouldn't have felt. While it pierced my side, it wanted to give me a high five. A congratulatory gesture on my conquests through the years that had me circling back around. It didn't sit right with me. A mellow, unsettling rumble in my stomach that tried to tell me something. Maybe that was why I hadn't been very inspired. Perhaps it was merely a coincidence.

But anyway it went, I felt this wasn't me. Maybe it was and still is, but not what I wanted. I'm healthy and full of vigor, but nights like that, especially the way it ended, and double for the way it could have ended, weren't giving me what I needed to do my job. What I needed to feel fulfilled.

I needed to know what I needed, what it was that would help make me not feel that way. Make me not feel like my life was missing something, except it was. And it had been missing for so long.

The taxi I hailed down had a rooftop advertisement. Something that I usually wouldn't have noticed, but I did because of its content: an ad for Florida vacations.

CHAPTER 9

So

The rain relentlessly beats down on me. I try to keep cover, but conditions aren't letting up and the wind, in all its anger, pushes everything side to side, again and again. As my thoughts turn back to the present, the realization that Viv is out in this weather to pick up my naked ass both warms my insides and has me scared for her well-being. *Why would she do this for me?* Maybe she's just a caring soul. Maybe there's something more to it all that I just don't see. But seeing as she's lived here longer than I, if she feels okay out here, then she probably is.

The past events of the day have been what I was looking forward to for countless nights. Years. There's something in me that is comparing what I thought would transpire versus what actually manifested in her room. There was a sense of romance, the style of romance as we know it. It was amazing, yet somehow at the end of it all, I still wound up outside, naked, and wet. Perhaps even the end of our tryst was how it was meant to end. Our own unique brand of romance, at least for the time being.

The wait for Viv is much shorter than I thought it would be. Either that, or my thoughts of New York take much longer than I realize. But either way, I see her pull up, cutting through the rain, my savior in an old, rusted silver BMW, no topper ads of Florida vacations. Past the furious tears from the sky that pound the windshield and the wiper blades racing back and forth, I see her laughing at me. Open-mouthed and enjoying the fruits of her drive. A good sign in all of this and I am happy she is enjoying this moment, at least for the laugh of it. I run to the car, keeping what I can covered up and hop in.

Inside, I sit on the sandy brown leather seats, stitches that are starting to fray at a few of the seams. Even a knob on Viv's radio has fallen off. Her laughter has picked up and tinted her face a lovely rouge. Her hands motion between herself and myself, unsuccessfully attempting to wave off the hilarity she finds in the moment.

She tries to chime in while wiping away a tear of laughter. "What the…"

But with a childish grin, I quickly interject, "Don't ask."

She notices my eye, causing the laughter to quell a few notches. She reaches out for it, to soothe the redness still present from before.

"Are you okay? It's starting to bruise."

"Oh, that? A fist fell into my face," I say, trying to make light of the situation.

Her laughter slows to a halt, but her mood is still light and enjoyable.

"A couple of times I see." She moves my head around, trying to get a better look. I doubt she's a nurse or anything, but she drove here, so she gets to examine.

She continues, "I don't suppose this has anything to do with why I am picking you up naked?"

"You suppose correctly. Long story," I say.

"We don't owe each other anything," she replies, leaving well enough alone.

"You're not far from here, are you?" I ask, already thinking I know the answer.

"Nah, not too far. I assume you do want to, and need to, come back to my place?" she says.

Though I'm not sure if she has any hidden intentions with that question, I don't want to worsen the storm.

"If you have clothes I could wear." I point to my birthday suit.

"Yeaaahhh." She draws out in a negative response to my inquiry. "It's me and my roommate. Her clothes are nowhere near your size. No worries though. Either way."

She says, "No worries," but I do worry because judging by how fast she made the drive here, my place is much farther. And I don't want her driving in this any more than she must. But what should I do? Try to fit into some T-shirt that, while oversized on someone who's 5'4" and weighs a buck fifteen, is going to make me look like some pansexual, unsure of his own pansexuality fitting into a muscle-tee three sizes too small.

So

She stops at a crossroads. No cars around as the rains punish the streets, flooding the drainage grates. Trees bend in the wind. A congratulatory bow to me and my situation, either that or to her and her kindness to brave this storm. Or both. The streetlights blink yellow. I can't help but think three things at this moment. One, I've been down here for a while now, and I still haven't seen any alligators. Living outside of Florida for all my life, you are made to believe alligators are an ever-present threat, ready to chomp down on you at any given moment. That is wrong and more than disappointing. Two, I want to be with her, though the face of her changes with each flash of lightning that paints the horizon in magnificent hues of yellows, oranges, and purples. Viv one flash; Faith another. My mind is unable to decide. Stuck. Always knowing that I want to be happy but never able to let myself be happy in the now, only in the possibility of what could be. One such option is Viv and me in bed, exploring each other in ways unable behind bushes. And three, the crossroads in front of me, both literal and symbolic. The big what to do, who to choose. Is this night, this moment, the answer to that question or am I overthinking the whole situation?

"So?" She nudges me.

I respond with a raised eyebrow and half-cocked smile. "Got a bath towel I could borrow?"

She makes a left turn and before I can delve deep into thought on anything or even space out, we pull up to a one-level house: gunmetal gray on the outside with what, in the light of the late night, appears to be off-white trim. The black skies make it look more like a house out of a Tim Burton film than a place you'd want to live in, but I can tell in the light of day it has pleasant curb appeal, despite the bushes and trees blowing in the hurricane winds.

There's a tan Ford Taurus in the driveway.

Viv turns to me with an unsure face. "I didn't know she'd be home."

"Seems to be the theme of the evening," I quip.

She catches the not-so-subtle hint at the night's events. "I thought she was at her guy's place."

"No worries," I reassure. "I can keep myself covered until I have a towel. We're all adults."

She laughs and makes a reference to one of the greatest sitcoms to grace television in the last four decades, "Sure about that, Naked Man?"

"I was not doing the Naked Man." I laugh out loud, impressed with her ode to *How I Met Your Mother*.

We dash out of the car and toward the door. About five feet into the rain, she drops her keys and fumbles for them on the ground. There is a look on her face, a mix of frustration and amusement at the moment. And it's the look on her face, as it's being beaten by the rain, that makes her look smokey. Her hair, wet and stringy, lays across her cheeks as she rises up. She sees me watching her. I urge her to finish the race to the door as I do a little dance, a dance that inspires urgency in her and that says, "'Hey, I'm naked here!" She laughs at my short jig and reaches the door.

Inside, the living room has a nice entertainment center with a well-kept, but older, tube television. The opposite wall has an eclectic assortment of framed movie posters, below which, an old plaid couch sits. A very surprised roommate perks up from her zoned-out state, turning from her late-night infomercial. Viv exits down a hall, hopefully to fetch a towel for me. There's a moment of awkward silence as her roommate stares at the naked man who just walked through the front door. She's deer-in-headlights-frozen, eyes fixed upon my scantily covered crotch. I outstretch one of my hands, which reveals a small spot of well-man-scaped pubic hair. She yawns as her eyes widen and shift to my hand for a quick second before shouting. "Viv, did you get a late-night stripper surprise? Cause I'm down for a stripper!"

"Finn," I say, hoping she says something else.

Nope.

"Are you a stripper?" Her excited anticipation causes a slight quiver in her voice.

She is cautious to shake my hand, unsure of what my next move may be. Like I am going to move my other hand and start flapping my penis side to side, shaking water off while singing, "Hello, My Baby."

"No. I'm not but thank you for the compliment."

"Name's Izzy," she replies. "Whatcha packin'?"

"I'm sorry?" I'm taken aback by her question. Not offended or anything, just shocked that she asked.

"Whatcha packin' there, big guy? You walk in covered only by rain and your hands, and now just hands, but you're not a stripper. I see you're in good shape. You groom nicely. So, the only thing that remains is... What. Are. You. Packing?"

I look her up and down. She is a complementary contrast to the rocker chick-meets-Harley Quinn-inspired color and style of Viv. Izzy has smooth

Mochaccino skin with dark, almost black eyes, a slight wave to her hair that gives it an "I'm always DTF" look. Her slender, defined jawline, high cheekbones, and perfectly pouty lips give her a natural look that is a balance of sweet meets "*I'll rock your world in ways you have yet to imagine.*" Decadent deliciousness and troublesome temptation all rolled into one.

Before I can get an answer out, a brown, ratty, old towel hits me, causing an instinctual grab for it as it hits the floor.

I grab it and cover myself, though Izzy has already seen the goods.

"Nice find, Viv. Where'd you get this one?" She says this as if I'm not even in the room anymore.

"Hands off, Izzy," Viv demands.

"Wasn't grabbing," Izzy defends.

"She wasn't. I let go to grab the towel, and she got a peek," I add.

Viv returns to the room with another small towel so I can dry myself.

"I found him behind the bushes," Viv illustrates.

"Oh yeah! I was there. Now I remember you. D.B. was talking you up to everyone. You're that producer guy."

"Guilty," I confess.

Viv grabs my hand and leads me to her bedroom. As her skin touches my palm, a thought enters my head. Of the man and his kingdom, of getting what you want out of life. She takes me by the hand down the hall, but my mind is frozen. Something edges in my brain about the machine and its beauty. The incalculable man hours spent building, tearing down, operating, setting up fireworks, selling goods, preparing food, interviewing, managing, bag checking, and more: all to put on a show so glorious that the worries of adulthood slip away. Prejudice, hatred, politics, finances, lost loves, deaths, everything. Gone. And so is my thought.

She closes the door to her room and smiles at me. I smile back, but all I can think about is where that thought was leading. She says something to me as she starts to undress. I really wish I heard her, but my mind is elsewhere, ever searching for the right thing at the wrong time. What sort of man thinks about a theme park when a wonderland is standing in front of him?

This guy. Obviously.

And it's not something I enjoy. It's something that is–a consuming cycle in my mind that won't quit until the answer is found. I hope that I can be here in this moment with Viv. Tend to her needs while tending to mine.

I snap back to the moment as her shirt hits me, covering my head. I remove it and catch the letters G 'n R on it. Nice pick. I flip the shirt around to read the message, "Get In The Ring, Mutherfucker." Double nice pick. And point taken.

For the moment, I shove aside the nagging search for my lost thought and be in service to her.

She is already lying on her queen-size bed, ready to doctor the wounds on my head and whatever else she may find. And I am prepared to let her.

I have never seen her before in all her beauty. We never made it this far behind the bushes, even though we went so much further in other ways.

I look her over as she does me, her beautiful body lying in the middle of her bed. The majesty of her perky breasts, nipples erect. A good sign for me. Her stomach's smooth, soft skin waiting to be gently kissed. I make my way to the bed and slide next to her. Moving in, our lips touch and embrace. Tongues dancing the tango. My hand reaches for her inner thigh, a spot I'd like to still further explore. I slide it up and stop at her black lace panties. I hesitate for a moment for some sort of confirmation.

"It ended this morning," she whispers in my ear.

Good enough for me. I slip a finger between the waistband and her skin. I feel Viv quiver as my nail glides across her flesh the length of the waistband to stop mid-stomach. She takes an intense, shallow breath as I move my hand back to her inner thigh. I rest my hand on her panty line. My thumb wraps upward as the other four fingers lay where her leg meets her dreamland.

As we play with each other, making our naughty nighttime dreams a reality, there is a soft knock at the door. Gentle rasp against the wood, begging for an invite inside. At this moment I am under her, but not yet inside her. She sits up and turns toward the door. The handle rotates, taking care not to disturb us as it opens. Izzy stands in the partially opened door. Her head peers through. Shirt off and bra on, as if she is anticipating a yes. This situation has played out for me before, the woman I'm with and her friend. A fun, frolic of a ménage-à-trois, but as Viv turns back to give Izzy her expected answer, I spy a look in her eye that says she doesn't want this tonight. But before she

So

answers Izzy, she turns to me, sweaty, naked, beautiful. Exposed. She looks at me and smiles a meek smile. Forced but trying to hide the fact she wants me for herself. Not because she is selfish, but because this is more to her than the others. In an instant, I'm back in college, pre-wunderkind of a musician but a whore nonetheless, in bed with that girl. The one who made me realize I'm that guy. Who told me she "wasn't usually like this" and wasn't. And as much as I've still been the same situationally accidental douche since, I don't want to be tonight. I can see it in her eyes. A desperate stare, trying to stay cool and hip. She wants me. Not just for unlawful carnal knowledge's sake, but for all of me. And I find myself taken by that. I shake my head just enough that she knows I'm hers. That tonight belongs to us.

CHAPTER 10

Growing Into You

F rom the moment I saw Viv in her Van Halen T-shirt, I knew she was trouble. I am twelve years her senior, but there is a connection, a spark that revs my engine in a way I've not felt before, or in so long I've forgotten. Not just sexually. Yes, my loins long for her in ways that make me want to be the white silk shirt hanging off one shoulder man with the wind blowing his hair back on the cover of some cheese-tastic mental masturbation novel. But there was something more. A feeling that this phenomenon we call life isn't overrated, is worth sharing with someone. Sure, this could all be the endorphins flooding my brain and making me feel like a high school boy getting an upskirt glance at the head cheerleader he's crushed on all year. I don't care. It feels good. And all that aside, maybe this is what life's all about. The great answer to the cosmic question. The existential relevance all great poets look for. The internal struggle

Trent has been singing about since before Nine Inch Nails and *Pretty Hate Machine* when he was working with Exotic Birds and Option 30. Endorphins. Perhaps, just maybe, the science behind this doesn't make the existentialism of it all obsolete.

The hurricane finishes its demolition somewhere between the bedroom door closing for what was left of the night and opening in the morning. All is calm after the storm. The trees are still. The air is moist and silent. Cars drive by on I-4, but the noise seems less than usual, almost too calm.

After a night of doing it like they do on the Discovery Channel, picking me up some clothes and getting keys remade for my place, we decide to spend the day at the animal park, specifically not the park with the caged whales. I like my monkeys, giraffes, hippos, and lions. I see this park for what it is: overpriced food, animals fooled into being happy in the safety of their cages, and countless employees furthering the gilded-ness of the big D. And I don't care. I know the overpriced food helps keep those animals in a clean place and well fed. Yes, they still make a profit, but they never hid the fact they were a for-profit place. I don't care; I love all of this. I decide to put my heart in her hands, metaphorically speaking of course. With her, there is a sense of comfort, of ease. A feeling that things will be okay. It is new for me to feel calm. Calm and relaxed is not something I do well. I tend to feel uneasy when I try to relax, like there's always a sense of something not being right. But here, with her, at this moment, I feel relaxed, and I am content with that.

As I said, the hurricane had passed, and the calm is here. Maybe that's what I'm feeling, the calm after the storm. While I hope it is not just that and something more, I'll enjoy it while it lasts if it is. The storm has passed, and she's still here.

We walk to an area that has Tamarin monkeys. Hell if I know what exact kind of monkey, but these things are the best. Tiny, little guys with puffy white hair on their heads that remind me of an early nineties rock star. These guys are awesome. We sit watching the animals in the cage that the park built, and the tiny rock stars seem content: swinging from branch to branch, grooming themselves, scavenging for bugs in between feeding times. They are a reminder of everything I could have been had I chosen differently back then, everything that most people are. Hell, in a sense, even what I've become. Someone who is comfortable in a routine. While the monkey's idea of every day may not be what the daily grind is to us, it's their little world. Just as we get up, shit, shower, shave, eat a quick breakfast, go to work, come home, and repeat five days a week, these guys do this day in and day out. Hell, I do what I do day in and day out. But this little set-up is a reminder that I am who I am, in spite of that. I wouldn't have met Viv if it wasn't for my own sense of routine and my need to break it.

I turn to her, to stare at the beauty I have quickly become fond of. She stares at the monkeys, a smile on her face. She entwines her arm in mine, giving it an endearing squeeze, a nonverbal thank-you of sorts for the day. I squeeze back, not you're welcome, but a thank-you. Thank you for staying the other night to meet me; thank you for last night; thank you for the sincerity that is Viv.

I know this must seem like I'm some half-aquatic fifteen-year-old redhead who falls in love with a boy while he plays with his dog, even though she has never actually spoken to him and has no idea if he's a complete asshat or not. Spoilers: He (kind of) is, and so is she. But this, right here, is new. And while I'm not falling in love, nor are my feelings close to that, I'm just enjoying it and the feeling it brings. Keeping an open mind about where things could lead.

We decide that tomorrow she's going to take me to the other side, the more grown-up version of what this city was built on. The inevitable follow-up to a park that is perhaps too family-friendly. We find ourselves at Universal. We arrive sometime as the sun sets, not exactly sure, but I don't care either way. All I can do as I look around City Walk, a delightful mix of restaurants and shopping—neither of which screams tourist—is think, *Is this how the other half lives?!* The tattoo shop here actually has some phenomenal artists, not just filler artists to grab the tourist's money. The selection of food is impressive. Burgers, sushi, seafood, and you can even waste away again in Margaritaville. A performer entertains atop a fifteen-foot-high servo driven stilt. A Steampunk restaurant. This place is so inviting without any pretense—if only the town were built on this venue instead.

It is so beautiful. Attention is given to every little detail inside and out, so much more than the gilded land of D. And this, of course, has me thinking, *Is there something I've been missing out on all these years? Have I been wallowing in something that I could have had if only I chosen a different path, a path that seemed, on the outside at least, less appealing?* I don't know, and I don't want to think about it. I try to stop the internal cycle of torment before it grips me too tightly and enjoy the day at a most amazing place.

The more I look around this area that I now live in, Orlando and all it encompasses, the more inspired I feel. The more I want to write songs of substance, not just the pop, (God forbid I say it) generic money-makers I moved down here to get away from. I'm sure Linda Perry can relate. After all, she left 4 Non Blondes, and after years of writing chart-topping songs, she started Deep Dark Robot to write stuff of more substance.

I look around at the Dr. Seuss section and it brings me back to childhood. Bright-eyed and wanting to run from statue to statue and building to building just to be a part of it all.

Viv watches as I do precisely that, the excited eight-year old I momentarily am. "Having fun, are you?" She giggles, enjoying the moments with me.

"Yes! This place is amazing!"

She smiles and lets out a belly laugh. "I'm glad you're enjoying yourself."

And the thing is, I am enjoying myself. At the park for the rest of the day and the following days together, I enjoy myself. I find myself in her company, and not much else matters. I know I still have a record release party to finalize, as well as the rest of the record to help with, but as I've said, I can't do my job if I don't feel inspired. Viv is doing just that, inspiring me and finding new ways to stimulate me.

Great songs, great books, great movies: all of them written by people who were inspired by someone, thus inspiring them to write said medium. No song was written without outside inspiration. So, even the muses need muses of some sort, and that's what's happening right now. She is amusing me. And it is glorious.

It's been a while since the storm, and I find myself happy to be in her company and her happy to be in mine still. Sometimes new flames, like fireworks, die quickly after a huge explosion. But sometimes, flames start strong and get stronger.

But here's the thing. Here's always the thing. The notion that has always been on my mind for years and now more than ever is there, festering in front. An itch I need to scratch but can't reach. A fly that buzzes in my ear that I can't swat away. Faith. God damn if I want to be thinking about her right now, but I am. Not just about our long overdue night together, but about the days since. The fact I haven't heard from her; the fact that in the few attempts I've made to call her in the few moments I've been without Viv, Faith has not answered. The fact that her overgrown man-beast of a boyfriend Ronnie had such a temper with me I don't know if she's okay. But she is an adult and has survived these many years without me; I try to let things rest. But allowing a sleeping dog to lie is harder than it seems. If only in so much as our urge to pet something so beautiful and peaceful, not to stir it but to try and add to its slumber. Except that petting a dog only stirs it. And once it wakes, there's no telling if it will be happy, tired, hungry, or worse, angry that you woke it.

While we currently sit at our favorite day-of-the-week-restaurant-haunt, I feel the buzzing of the fly at my picnic. I don't want this to happen. The restaurant is littered with a few tables of people eating and enjoying their day. The whole environment is in good spirits. Viv and I are just enjoying a few drinks. But I feel the tickle in my ear of the flapping wings and high-pitched biz-buzz sounds: Jeanine.

Entering in through the side patio door, wearing a blue-and-white tie-dyed sundress and sandals to match, she saunters to the bar as if she hasn't a care in the world or a thought in her mind. But I see it in her eyes. She has an idea, and she's waiting for the right moment to release it into the world, to stir up whatever she feels like stirring.

Shoo fly, don't bother me.

But as a fly won't listen, neither will she. Jeanine ignores the expression on my face that displays anything but a welcoming tone. She sits down on my right, once again placing me between the two ladies. I didn't like the feeling before, and I sure as hell don't like it now. The urge to run screaming is rapidly tingling through my legs, an electrical impulse to carry me away from this inevitable disaster for my own safety. But I'm a man, and a man's past, no matter how small or annoying the part, is always his past, and if it collides with his present, the only person to point the finger at is himself.

"Tricky Finn! What an odd surprise to see you here!" Jeanine says in her most pleasantly sarcastic voice as she flags the bartender down for a drink.

Viv looks at me with a raised eyebrow. "So why does she call you Tricky Finn?"

Without me able to get a fraction of a word out, Jeanine chimes in, "Once, a long, long time ago, he did something stupid. Not stupid like idiotic. Just juvenile."

"I was a juvenile. Well, just past that stage anyhow," I defend myself.

"So, what's your excuse now, Finn?" Jeanine chimes in.

"Hey, Jeanine. He seems like a very mature man." Viv coming to my defense is a nice gesture, although I can handle myself.

"Really? Did he ever tell you why you had to pick him up in the middle of a hurricane with no clothes on and only his phone?"

Or not. Maybe I can't handle myself. Abort. Abort.

"Why, Jeanine? Why?" Yes. I'm pleading a little bit, but it seems the once annoying fly at the picnic has matured into a new species of annoyance and is hell-bent on ruining this for me.

"I just thought she should know you, Finn Fairlane. The real you. Like I do."

"You knew me many years ago."

"Judging by the parking lot blowjob and what Faith told me, you are still the same ole' Finn."

Viv is fidgeting in her chair, unsure of what's going on at the moment. "That was a nice moment between two consenting adults."

"Thanks, Viv. But this isn't about you. She is harboring some weird animosity toward me, and I don't know why. This isn't all just about open honesty, is it?"

"Do you have any idea what you've done to my sister?"

"What did you do to Faith? And why were you naked?" Viv chimes in, getting visibly shaken.

Fine. Jeanine wants my life laid out for Viv right here.

"I didn't do anything to Faith. I mean, not currently. We dated. Almost twenty years ago. She broke up with me. All those sappy breakup songs I wrote that played on the radio. All those songs over the years about love that you hold so dear. All for her. All about her. But she left me. Then I moved here, and here she was, is, whatever. And all these memories came rushing back. All these feelings came with them. And things happen. But I met you."

Viv interrupts, "Please tell me I am not just a way to kill time until she comes around on her feelings for you? Not just another woman for you to notch on your headboard?" It hits her, and a look of disgust washes over her face. "Did you just get done fucking her when I picked you up?! Did I sleep with you not hours after you just had your dick inside her? I know we didn't owe each other anything. We weren't exclusive. Maybe we still aren't. But I just figured some shenanigans. Not that you double dipped with me. Or just with me, but with *her* of all people! I honestly thought more of you than that. Hell, I thought you thought more of me! Fuck, more of her! How naïve I must be to assume you wouldn't do that to me? So, tell me it's not true, Finn!"

I don't want to respond. I don't want to lie. I'm an honest guy. I want to stay silent and not ruin this, but the look on my face, a look I didn't even realize I was making, says it all. Well, not all.

"No. No. Yes. I'm sorry." The only words to peep out of my unsure mouth.

Still kicking the dog when he's down, Jeanine interjects, "Finny boy. This is what happens when you avoid your duties. Had you just been writing, producing..." She pauses for dramatic effect that only agitates me more. "You wouldn't be in this mess," she finishes icing the cake that was her words.

"Seriously, Jeanine. That's your moral lesson here? I need to work more?"

"No. But when was the last time you met with Spear Fist? Last week?"

"Why the hell do you even care? What are you getting out of all this?" I desperately want to know. As this situation worsens, I need to find a card to play. An upper hand.

"Gregg is my boyfriend."

"Who?"

"The drummer."

"That's his name!" Not something I should have said out loud, but it came out before I could stop it.

"Seriously? What's your damage?" Jeanine does have a point. I should know all their names.

"Nothing. Just slipped my mind." No, it didn't. I'm just an ass sometimes. Maybe more than I intend.

"I want to see him, and Spear Fist, go far, even if it is because of you. And if it is your doing, I don't want your philandering ways to get in his."

"You couldn't have just come in here and said, 'Hey, the guys need you. Please see them?'"

"I could have, but this is much more a guarantee that now you will. That now you will make sure their record gets the attention it deserves and is due."

I would like to shout names at her. Mean, childish names unbecoming of a person my age, or any age really, but there is a part of me that respects her for doing this. That sees her as a tough, driven individual. As a person who can understand what it takes to get what she needs out of someone, not the annoying child she once was. The fly has mutated into some-thing new. Someone to reckon with, or not to. That phrase never did make much sense. Too bad I under-estimated her.

"Finn." The tone of Viv's voice is serious. The anger seems to have calmed down for the moment. "Was I just someone to pass the time? Someone to fill in the space until she calls you back?"

"No. I'm drawn to you. Your energy. Your spirit. I never thought it would go down this way."

"Why did you call me during the storm? Why me? Why not the band? Why sleep with me right after her?"

The answers to those are more difficult than she might think. To say that I don't know many people, and I knew she would answer her phone, seems like I used her for a ride. While there is some truth to that, it's not at all like that.

"I called you because Ronnie just beat the shit out of me, and I wanted to see you."

"For what? A healing BJ?" Viv is obviously not seeing eye to eye with me at this moment. Perhaps I should have been more upfront.

Jeanine laughs as she finishes her drink.

"No. As I said, I like you. Did from the first night." I say this, and it's true, but it's one of those things that will always sound like a line from someone trying to save face.

"I'm not sure, Finn."

"Be as unsure as you want. But I wanted to see you. You. Not anyone else. I didn't call up D.B., bragging to him about the events. I didn't try to lure Faith outside to get my clothes or even my car keys. I called you. It's the same reason…" While lost in my answer, I had almost forgotten that Jeanine was right there. Almost. So, my voice softens. I'm not one to have shame about things, but private things are private. "It's why I said no to Izzy."

Jeanine pipes up in her chair as she sips her drink a la some crappy Audrey Hepburn imitator. "Excuse me? I didn't quite hear that."

Viv turns to Jeanine as she tries to collect her mannerisms. "Please shut the fuck up. You've done enough."

Jeanine stands up huffing as she sets her glass down. "I came here on your side, Vivian. But if you think otherwise, I can leave."

I take this moment for myself to try and preserve my dignity, or what's left of it. "I think that would be best."

Viv whips back around to me. "You've lost your say in this."

The ear-to-ear smile that crosses Jeanine's face is wiped away just as fast as it came as Viv says. "He's right though. Leave."

Jeanine storms off. "You know, Finn, if you put as much time into your clients as you do screwing up your love life, you'd still be famous."

The sting of her words, blunt as they may be, stab sharp, mainly because she might be correct. But be that as it may, wallowing is not my thing. At least about that. So as the silence drowns us for the moment after Jeanine's departure, I try to tread the waters and let my mind clear.

"If you didn't want to screw this up, you sure as shit did a good thing badly."

"So goes the story of my life. But at least I trudge along and try to do it right."

She smiles a little smile. If she weren't trying to hold it back, it would be so much bigger and so beautiful, but it is this shy smile that caught my eye and heart in the first place.

"What do you want me to say?" It's not a great thing to say, but it's all that comes to my mind. I'm at a loss for words. Honesty wasn't a home run, and neither was withholding the truth. And of course, with the middle ground long past missed, I am at a loss for words. So, I ask her.

But her immediate response is silence. An unsettling silence: the kind that all the fiber of your being knows is not going to be broken with kind words. A silence so tense that dare it breaks may cause nuclear-level explosions. But all I can do is sit and hope I'm not the trigger that sets it off.

Watching her search for her words is not beautiful. It is scary. There are not a lot of women who could have done this to me. There's Faith. And one more in the time between Faith and now. That's it. And now there's Viv. I am not that man anymore. I can't be the one who walks away uncaring, unphased, unscathed. Not from her. I have my scars, and I wear them like a badge of honor. I am who I made me and I'm okay with that. But I don't want to add to her wounds any more than I have this day. So, I'm sitting. Waiting. There is a part of me that hates that I allowed myself to fall for someone so quickly, that I allowed myself to get close. But I did, and a larger part of me does not hate it, does not want it to be different.

The center of her lips begins to open. The silent tension dissolves without explosive effect, more like a torrential downpour that, in an instant, hushes without cause. There is a suspicion in that silent tension that something worse is yet to come.

"I want you to say nothing. You and Jeanine have said enough." She stabs me with her words.

"Then what can I do? What do you need from me?"

I always felt those were desperate words to use, but after asking for the words to say and that being her response, I succumb to a submissive role for the moment.

"Time."

A harsh, one-word response to shut me the hell up and stun me. Not that I can't move. I'm just so unsure of what move to make that my mind won't move my body, which is doubly not fun as I don't even respond to her rising from her seat and walking away. I just stare across the bar as she exits out the patio door and disappears off into the same viewpoint as she did when we first found each other in the bushes.

Still, I'm stunned.

CHAPTER 11

Dream On

E ven D.B. and the rest of Spear Fist feels a stronger connection to Badaboom. The magic power of the hurricane brings everyone closer to what's important to them in some mystical, cosmic way. Neil and Vincent have come together on their riffs in a very coupled way. Gregg seems less distanced from the band, which is nice considering what Jeanine did for him. Maybe it's because of what she did for him. Jeanine is either going to be a proverbial Yoko to Lennon or Dorothea Hurley to Bon Jovi. If she's some incarnation of Hurley, then I welcome it, but if she's a Yoko, then I shall destroy her.

They've had two meetings as a band without me in the time since the storm, and both have accomplished what I hoped: ideas born and breathing on their own. The best thing about their coming together is that both practices have been without me, which, surprisingly, is my end goal. To help things get to a better place. To get a band to a mindset where they want me around instead of needing me. The devil's in the details of the difference between the two.

So far, this third meeting, with me in attendance, is no different. The energy buzzing around the studio is contagious, full of creativity from all sides and a healthy exchange of ideas. This session was the most cohesive I've seen them since I first started working with them. Instead of turning every little idea into an argument, causing backward progress, they are listening, offering insights to enhance ones already given instead of new ones that negate the original. The band acts as a sounding board to better each song as a whole, not trying to force-fit pieces together. To me, at least, this is how people create fun music.

We all sit around, instruments in hand, discussing ideas for the last song to be written, the opener. Without a solid opener and a killer closer, which they already have, the album, any album really, is just a collection of forgettable songs. A strong opener makes the following songs tie together—whether musically, lyrically, or telling an epic story. And the closer brings it all together, an exclamation mark on the album. We need the opener. The record release party is a few weeks away, and we still need to record this one last song, mix it down, and press the albums. As anyone in the industry knows, that's a lot to do in very little time.

Gregg gets up from his drum set and lights a hookah. This is no ordinary hookah either. It has five three-foot hoses, one for each bandmate and an extra for guests. The design of the hookah itself is what makes this puppy special. The blown glass body

was fired specifically for the band. The base of the
water pipe is a fist. Stemming from that is a spear-
head embedded into the top of the hand and spear
rising from there, with red glass bleeding out of the
wound. The whole thing, except for the blood, col-
lects the resin, changing color until cleaned; that, however, is not near often enough. But always fresh water
in the base.

We start passing it around, adding fuel to the
already creative fire. We were talking about intro
tracks. There were already eleven songs on the album,
not counting the opener.

D.B. chimes in, "Iowa."

Gregg retorts, "You want us to cover Iowa?"

"I assume he means do a similar intro. Dark, heavy,
and cryptic in sound and voice," I chime in, wanting to
prevent a derailing of the past few weeks' productivity.

A ten-ton hammer of an idea smacks me across
the face, bringing the searing smarts of Ronnie's fist
fresh to the front of my mind again.

Give them "I Will Build My Cross."

There is a school of thought out there that old writ-
ings are old and always write fresh lyrics for fresh
music. Never revisit old sets. I can understand that
mindset. If it's old, by the time acceptable music is
written for it, the verses may be outdated, outgrown,
or just below current talent levels. But sometimes an
old set sticks around. I feel like this is one of them.

Keep it a soft, spoken word intro over music: slow,
fast, in between, it doesn't matter. We'll figure that out
quickly. But for now, the lyrics. The rising tide of the

album. The introduction dripping with sarcasm that
starts Spear Fist's latest, greatest album ever.

We are the crucified
Not those who live in
Cold, cardboardboxes,
or who walked into
Shower rooms
turned ovens
We are the crucified.
With roofs, beds, and food on our tables. Our wounds attended
to at the push of 911 or 976. They are not the crucified. Those
who left their homes being promised a better life, not knowing that
was death. We are the crucified because it is our blood that runs
red. Our cries that are heard. Not theirs. Theirs run clear because
no one is there to see it run red. No one hears them cry. No one
cares. Not anymore.
We crucify ourselves.
They do not.
They want the pain
And the hunger.
The frostbite.
Infections. Disease
and the ridicule.
They suffer from
h o m e l e s s n e s s
genocide, mass
incarcerations and
being subhuman
because they are
humble. If this is true,
Then crucify me
And forgive me
for I know not what I do.
For I will buy some
wood. And
commission a cross.
And then
I will crucify myself.

As I finish reading the lyric set, the guitar is already strumming something that resonates of a diminished minor. The sad sound of forlorn, isolated, desperate solitude fills the room. A kick drum starts in, followed by a soft, military-style drum roll on the snare. The bassist sits, listening, mentally writing the bass line. I see him air bass out a minimalist riff, something to drone in the background. It already sounds perfect to me. The drum roll turns into a beat. The guitar picks up momentum.

From my pocket, my phone vibrates and buzzes a few bars of "In-A-Gadda-Da-Vida": my "I don't have you programmed in my phone so why the hell are you calling me?" ringtone. I am hoping for a call-back though. The record release party is quickly approaching, and I'm still hoping for news from my contact. Everything they have under their belt is good, if not great. But it's been under-publicized and under-rated. I want this album to get the attention it deserves. Maybe it's fate lending a hand.

"Hello. Fairlane speaking."

I listen to the other end of the phone as the guys all stare at me. As of now, the release party is at a microbrew bar in an indoor marketplace. It reminds me of a permanent expo booth set up, but with good shit. Big enough for a sizeable stage. Live sound is always finicky and always a gamble. But it's live music, so I don't much care about that. Fans will hear them, people who haven't heard them will become fans, and all will buy their album and support local businesses. This will be the event. Food enough for everyone to play into Romanesque stereotypes of gluttony and misconceived vomitoriums. Beer aplenty to make sure this brewing company stays on the map and not just makes an appearance.

She talks for a moment and I listen intently. A smile slowly starts crossing my face. The guys all have the same quizzical look on their faces that beg to know why the hell I am smiling. From the pot, perhaps. Yes, but no. This is more.

"Sounds perfect. Original date still?" I ask.

The guys are getting excited and start joyously laughing for reasons they don't yet know.

"Perfect. This will be huge. I'll be by tomorrow with the deposit," I assure my contact. "Thank you so much."

I hang up and find the band staring at me with a mix of "What the fuck" and "Dude, we aren't done yet" carved into their stoned faces.

I yell to the gods above, "We got the amphitheater!"

The guys start in with a chorus of cheers. And I let them enjoy the moment before I bring them back down to reality.

"The opener, guys." A sobering reminder that deadlines approach.

The fleeting moment of joy has passed, and they quickly sober up.

"How do you do it, man?" D.B. asks, presumably of my booking the dream location.

"I make phone calls," I deadpan.

"Not that. The music, Finn. How do you write what you write?"

The look on my face and the pause in my answer must have given away more than I intended. I'm not sure how to answer in one conversation what I've been writing about and trying to explain myself for decades. I don't want to lie to D.B., and this moment isn't here to brush him off. Actors pull from the deepest, darkest emotions they have to shoot hard scenes. This, in relation to musicianship, is a hard scene. I don't want to fake this.

"D.B., you have that girl, the one that got away. I'm sure everyone in this room has that one. But it's more than just a failed relationship," I start.

They have given me their full attention. Vincent has stopped strumming. Neil has put the hookah pipe down and exhales his last hit. No feedback drones in the background. Gregg sets down the sticks he was using to tap out beats on his thighs. Every ounce of attention is on me.

"You have to be willing to destroy yourself in order to make something far greater than just you. You have to be willing to destroy relationships, almost con- sciously. Like a speeding train toward a stalled car on the tracks. You see it happening, and no matter how hard you pull the brakes, it's too late. There will be blood. There will be pain. And there will be destruction. But unlike the train and the car, our odds of walking away are much better. It's in how we deal with it. It's that we deal with it that makes our music. Makes something much greater than we could ever be individually."

D.B. interjects, "But she's back in your life. Can't you have it all now?"

And while that is a great question, the obvious answer of yes is far too simple to be accurate. Or ever the answer.

"Faith is the greatest love I have ever known. The greatest inspiration for all my writing, in the past and now. A part of my heart has ached since we first went our separate ways all those years ago and still aches to this day. Wanting, yearning to be with her. To be with her, in her presence, is to be in the presence of greatness."

"Then what's stopping you?" D.B. prods for more.

"We hold onto things. Memories. Ideas of what once was and what could have been. Like a high school sweetheart that went astray or crush you never dared to approach. You hold onto manufactured ideas of what you thought the future would be like or who the person was in your mind and of a relationship never had."

Gregg goes to speak up but coughs a bit. A break in the tension. "Hmm. But wait. You did have her. Had a relationship."

"Yes. And we all went to high school, and college, and the memories are there. You can't go back. No one is the same as they were then. No matter what they say. So, the relationship we had then is there, in the past. To start it again would not be to pick up where we left off like no time has passed, and nothing happened in the between."

D.B. lights up, a sobering, buzzkill of a moment. "You would have to treat it as new. Learning to see if it would work this time around or end worse than last time."

A wink at him and tap my finger on my nose. "There it is. And the songs of the minstrels, bards, and lyricists of times past are not actually about the reality of the relationship. They are about the romanticized concept of what the relationship is or was."

Vincent clears his throat, a voice I've heard only a few times in the past month. "And to try again could ruin what you have to write with."

I wish he weren't wrong. He is, but not fully. There's always a part of a writer that doesn't want to ruin the illusion of what he or she is romanticizing. The rose-colored glasses give them the fuel to write. To pull back the curtain and reveal the tiny man behind it doesn't make for a great story. Just a great moment in it. But on the other hand, magic is only cool if you know how they pull off the trick and you can still find it magical.

It's a conundrum for the ages, more so than to be or not. Or being with the one you love or loving the one you're with. It's about starting over with the one you used to love to see if the love is still there. Being open and vulnerable, once again, to the person who, once upon a time, tore your world asunder.

So, when D.B. asks, "Can I have it all?" the only honest answer is, "I don't know." All I can do is try to understand where and how everything fits together.

The events of that meeting bled over into the next few days of recording track after track to get the sound just right. But unlike my first month here, I find myself now wanting to turn up the snare and adjust the low frequencies of the bass drum and floor toms. Tweaking the equalization on the guitar to get the notes ringing crisp and clear before throwing the right amount of fuzz, distortion, and overdrive onto it to give Spear Fist the sound that will push them beyond famous.

Here's the rub, though. I wouldn't be in the mindset I am if it weren't for everything I've been through since moving down to Florida. I would have influenced the band differently if things happened differently. The end sound of the album would not be what it is if I hadn't irked Jeanine into what she did because her mood and perspective on the situation affected Gregg and his input into it. D.B., Vincent, and Neil would also have contributed differently if their lives were influenced differently. Some may say that the whole feel of the album is happenstance, since it's based on the events that preceded. While not entirely wrong, it's not right either. The overall feel of the album is decided long before the events of our lives transpire, but the way it is put together—the dark, sullen tones or bright guitar solos, the use of a droning bass line or something more akin to John Myung, if D.B. is going to have angry vocals or just the other side of vengeful—those are all influenced by the events in our lives.

And here's the funny thing: While what happens to each of us every day may be coincidental, the way we handle them is what changes how these incidents affect us.

CHAPTER 12

Separate

L ife becomes a pattern, no matter where you live. Everyone has a break from the daily grind, but even those become routine and become their favorite haunts. My life is no exception. Wherever I've lived, I have my favorite places. NYC was Sunswick. Chicago was Exit and Neo. In Orlando, it has become this restaurant, our restaurant. There's something about the patio, the way it is set up. It allows for groups to sit together without being segregated from others. The fire pit in the center of it all. This day though, it looks as if they also added fire pits on each end of the patio. Not the round kind on the ground. These are raised, in fish tanks, I would guess. Glass rocks cover the bottom. Propane-fueled. Very pretty works of functional art.

It is little things like that you notice at your favorite haunts. The idiosyncrasies of a loved one that only you know about. If I didn't frequent this place, I would not have noticed. I wouldn't have known it was new. And much like visiting my favorite haunt after a brief time away at a new locale, I'm here again, grabbing a quick drink as a cosmic thank-you for things coming together. Badaboom is finished. The albums are pressed. CDs printed. T-shirts made. And I must head over to the amphitheater. My contact is already in the middle of setting up, and I need to be too. It's nice right now—early afternoon. The patio is empty, save for one young couple eating fried cheese. A peaceful alternate from the nightly masses that gather.

But perhaps coming here tempted fate to smite me again. Maybe I should have had a drink at home and went straight to meet my contact. But fate has other ideas.

Fate has Faith.

All I want is some sense of normalcy for the day. It's too big a day, too much riding on this. Not just for me, but for D.B. and the rest of the band. Normalcy, for a while in my life. But I guess if you've led the life I've led, my normal isn't the same to anyone else. Normal is this, wanting a day free of drama and not getting it. Ever.

I get up to leave and somehow manage to make eye contact with Faith. Faith, who stands all the way at the opposite side of the bar. Past five rows of booths, tables, a bar, server station, and not to mention windows in dire need of cleaning, plus all the customers and staff inside. It would only be to my benefit if she sat facing away, so the gods have seated her facing me. She is speaking with the bartender. She has no man by her side. No sister. No killer bee buzzing around or walking mountain guarding her against the likes of me. Just her. A small ship in the storm of my life. *Why the hell is she here so early?*

I break eye contact and look back to the young couple sharing a chair meant for one still feeding each other sticks of fried cheese. It's not that I don't want to see her. I do, more than anything. But right now, I have to go to the record release party I set up. I have to call agents, managers, record labels, the people who make names. Get all the affairs in order, so it goes off without a hitch—all within a few hours. So, I can get their careers going up, up, up. I look back at Faith to wave goodbye. She doesn't wave back. She holds up a finger that universally means "Hold on a sec." For her, I'll wait a billion seconds. Always. But this timing is horrendous. I need to leave. I stay though. It's what I do. It's one of those little things about me. One of my idiosyncrasies, for better or worse.

But this might be what it is all about. What we musicians have been singing about since we first learned how to sing. The moments spent with loved ones, whether family or the friends we consider family, figuring out which people in our lives deserve the title of family, which people deserve to stay in our lives. Moments spent laughing and sharing stories. Raising a toast to memories of the past. To inside jokes. To the little idiosyncrasies that only those closest to that tight knit group knows. Raising our glasses and sharing a drink with those that not only know us best but accept all parts of us for who we are.

Idiosyncrasies. It fits, not just now but always. All places for all people. It is a perfect word. I feel a little like Mr. Rogers, and that's my word of the day. Say it with me, Idio-syn-cra-sies.

I watch her as she heads to me. Every time I see her, thoughts of my past race through my mind. All my regrets that led me to my present. She steps closer. All my mistakes that shaped who I am. She still steps toward me. All my loves. My loss. My ambitions. She steps closer again. My fears. Dreams. Hopes. This point. The now. The "why" that answers why I am here. The curiosity that led me by the hand my entire life. Disregarding the consequences of it all. Thinking only of the possible reasons my curiosity leads. The possible outcomes of the curious situation. That is why I am stuck standing here and not running to save my sanity. And my curiosity is answered.

She exits the restaurant. Her pitch-black hair, the perfect contrast to the lightning, is with her bright smile across her face. Short-sleeved shirt showing off her sleeved arm still vibrantly colored, but also a new work of art on her other arm, a piece that, like her hair, is inked in stark opposition. A black, shaded design of spider web and lace that starts from somewhere beneath her white V-neck T-shirt and trails off just past the elbow. The unscented, dye-free lotion hydrates it enough to glisten in the bright light of day. It brings about a newness in her. A far cry from the straight-haired, conservatively dressed young woman I first met all those years ago. A notch away from the grown woman I didn't recognize at the burger stand outside Old Town. There is this look in her eye as she smiles and heads my way. I don't know what the look means, nor if I should be excited to find out. Maybe I should be nervous. I am nervous. Anxious perhaps, but still, I know I am not getting out of hearing whatever her eyes have to say. Maybe I don't want to get out of hearing it. Maybe, just maybe, I am ready to listen to what her eyes are not able to speak.

She stops in front of me. We stare into each other's eyes, playing a game of chicken. The first one to speak loses, except I don't know what to say and I have to leave. I don't understand why she came out here to stare at me. I don't mind. There's sadness in this moment that makes me want to cry. *How did she know I'd be here? Did she spot me from inside well before I spotted her?* The look in her eyes moves to her lips, her cheeks tugging up the corners. Just enough that if you are looking for it, you'll see it. A moment later, she purses her lips, drawing in confidence to say what she needs. But as quickly as they tightened, they relax. She squints her eyes—a sign of disappointment in herself.

Without saying a word, she gestures with one finger for me to wait here. I raise an eyebrow in curiosity and nod my head. Off she walks behind the building. I let her do her thing and not spy. I pull out a cigarette and light it up, enjoying the inhale to calm my nerves because I have to leave.

Half a cigarette later, she returns with a reusable shopping bag in hand.

She tosses it at me, saying, "'Here."

I catch the surprisingly light bag and peek inside.

My clothes, keys, and wallet.

"I thought you might want them back eventually," she continues.

"I have to get to the amphitheater. The party's in a few hours," I whisper.

"I know," she says. "I'll be there too."

I may not have spoken first, but I lost the game. I'm okay with that. Faith smiles and stares into my eyes. Her mouth refuses to say what her eyes are screaming. I wish I were better at those eye-to-eye conversations. But I'm not. So, I wait. I wait for her to say something more: something like she regrets the last two decades, something like she's sorry she hurt me. But why would I want her to say those things? I don't regret the past twenty years. I'm not sorry she hurt me. My love for her, the love we had for each other shaped me, shaped my life to make me who I am. It gave me the life I have, and my life isn't a life to complain about—at least the nights and days I can remember.

Maybe she needs to tell me she's engaged. Some desperate attempt by Ronnie to mark his woman: to remind her not to have sex with me, to proverbially urinate all over her to ward off any other potential suitors who would otherwise make attempts to steal her for themselves.

A final goodbye, perhaps. Before sailing off into the sunset, forever lost at sea to me. But I don't want that. One can't simply just turn one's back on their history and pretend it never happened. Faith would have to lose her ink, strip her hair, go back to being the innocent, naïve girl she once thought she was, forget everything she has become.

So, I open my mouth to say something. But my mind is still unsure of what to say, which works out.

"Here comes Viv," she says.

I watch while she disappears back into the crowd at the bar, but I still have one eye on Viv as she sits near to me, all too aware of the peculiar events that just transpired. The look on her face is not kind.

But now I'm wondering what's next. The gods have told me once that I should have just drunk at home. I have to leave, and now Viv shows up. I don't mind that she's here. In fact, under normal circumstances, I would welcome the fact she is here, but I'm not sure why she's here too. And at noon, nonetheless. *Why the hell are people I know here at noon?*

"Thought you were at the theater?" she interrogates.

"Stopped by for a quick drink. It seemed fitting." *Why am I defending myself?*

"What's in the bag?" She pokes at it.

"Seems she wanted to give me back my stuff," I show her the bag.

"Clothes?" She tries not to seem jealous or intrusive.

"Just debris from the storm. Nothing important that wasn't replaced," I reply.

But it is—giving this back to me, not saying anything. Silence speaks louder than words sometimes. Interpreting what the silence means is a whole other story. I want to know why she sat there silently. I want to run inside after her but next to me now is a woman who offers herself openly. Viv drove through a hurricane for me. She is doing her best to be accepting of who I am and the past that has caught up to me.

And all I can think of is how I can't deal with the inquisition starting up right now. I have to go.

I look into Viv's eyes, and they desperately scream to me, "Stay! Don't run. There's so much more for you here than there. I've not hurt you and I won't." But at the same time, Viv is angry at what she thinks she saw. Angry and uncertain in the fact that she knows both her and Faith hold pieces of my torn heart. The silver lining she has in that lies in the fact we still have more uncharted territory than charted. There is no pain here, not yet anyhow. But her uncertainty also lies in the fact I'm not a big enough asshole to get up from one woman I am with to pursue the past and tumultuous present of another, she hopes, no matter how powerful the urge to do so maybe.

I have to leave.

"Why are you here?" I turn the phrase on her.

"I have to use the lady's room," she says, avoiding the answer. "Wait."

"I have to go meet my…" I start to say.

Viv interrupts, "Just wait a minute."

She heads inside and Faith emerges back out, a game of "Let's fuck with Finn" I don't have time to play.

"I left him," she starts.

I fall back in my chair. I stare at Faith with both wide and squinted eyes. A look that says, "You shouldn't have," yet at the same time begs, "Did you do it for me?"

"I didn't leave him for you." Well, that answers that rather quickly. She continues, "Don't even start there. I left him because it was time. He never was who I imagined myself with for long term. He was fun. He was a distraction." The reasons pour forth from her mouth.

I ask, curiosity piqued, "Distraction from what?"

"Life. You. This mortal coil." Her answers are curt.

I gaze at her for a moment. She sinks into a seat next to me as if saying that released the weight of a thousand worlds. But she still doesn't look happy; that gave her no solace to end things with Ronnie. She holds onto a look that foretells of a night ending very badly.

At least she isn't reminding me of every bad thing done. She is bittersweet. Like I may have meant more to her than I thought.

"And you were supposed to be just a distraction. It was supposed to be fun. It was not supposed to be this. What it was. When we met, I was using you. It was supposed to be simple," Faith says, all but confirming I am wrong about her feelings.

I feel like an asshole because I HAVE TO LEAVE. I am getting told everything I ever wanted to hear, and it should feel great—a should-be-joyous, momentous occasion but I HAVE TO LEAVE. The irony of Faith's words at this moment is "I'm not hurt nearly as bad as I thought I would be." Instead of dread or despair, I feel a sense of relief, not quite of joy. Almost relief. A sense of calm. As if my years of worry, my years of wondering, were all for nothing. Well, not nothing but rather unnecessary. The universe had my back in making sure she was okay, but the price to pay was mine.

Then she continues to tell me how it wasn't simple. It wasn't just her getting hers—at least after a while. It became something more than her selfishly fulfilling her needs. It became real. It became something she wanted, something she feared losing. But, like me, she too saw the inevitable end. Saw that our lives crossed but that road was coming to a close. That the departure would be painful and so she started distancing herself. She started keeping her distance before things got bad, I mean utterly bad, so that when they did, she could leave mostly unscathed.

"Did it work?" I keep my response short and simple. I don't want to turn this into a conversation that I fuck up, an honest chat about things that turns into hell because of my mouth.

She smiles, almost. She wants to; I can tell because her face tightens for a quick second, and it changes the look to a hint of happy.

Then she unloads, "I didn't like the fact that I used you. Yes, at first, I was okay with it. I wanted to feel something new. And you were there. I didn't like that I fell for you. But I did. I resented the fact that our paths had crossed at such a shitty time for both of us, but I stayed as long as I could. I didn't like most of what we had because of the situation. Not because of you. I've tried so many times to push you out of my mind. To make me not love you. To demonize you and make you into someone you're not. To believe the tabloid writers as if they spoke gospel because it would have made you much easier to hate. But I couldn't, I can't, and I don't know why our paths have crossed again, but I don't want them to split. Not again. Not now. I know you didn't keep yourself pure for me all these years, and I didn't do that for you. I lived my life after us, and I loved my life after us, but you're here, and I'm here, and we wouldn't be who we are had it not been for the other. So why forget all of that? Why push it all aside for possibilities that may not be? I know nothing is certain, even us, but I'd rather try us than not try at all. I'd rather bank on our past and our history. I can't guarantee this would work anymore than I could have thought back then that I'd be who I am today. But I'm here, Finn. You're here. That's gotta mean something."

I want to run to her through a field of lilies into each other's arms and hug forever. But that's not us, nor is it real. What's real is my muse, the love of my life, the woman who shaped me just confessed the weight she's been carrying for so long. She admitted everything, and she knows that I'm content with Viv. I'm satisfied with my current situation, short and new as it may be. I'm happy. There are no rock star nights of endless drugs and meaningless sex with strangers forgotten in the next day's blur. And I'm content now. Yes. I love Faith. Yes, Faith will always be my one. She will always hold the biggest place in my heart.

She will always be "that girl."

Do I wash away the foundation I'm building with Viv? Do I ignore my short time here, great as it was? Just write it off as filler, something to pass the time until Faith hopefully calls? I have a beautiful woman who accepts me for who I am, for what I am. She doesn't judge my past, but believes in the now and the future. A woman who wants to be with me. A woman who inspires me to be better. A woman whose history with me is untainted, mostly. A woman who seems to want to build a future with me.

But Faith sits before me. *Should I have known that it would have led to this? How could I have known?* As fucked up as it is, all three of us here just past noon, I somehow should have known. It is just this. And it seems that *la fortes del destino* have brought me to this, to this moment.

She stops speaking and her eyes shift to the sky above, searching the heavens for what's next.

She leans forward and kisses me. Not a hot and heavy, "Let's go behind the bushes" kiss. This is a kiss I have never felt before. A real "My hand to God" kiss filled with real emotion, love even. I hold her head in my hands. We share a kiss filled with both solace and sadness, excitement and calm. I feel myself shaking. I shake, tremble, quiver, and it feels scary. I feel like I might explode. The world around me ending in a fiery death caused by my explosion. I hear everything. The sound of her lips on mine. The sound of my heartbeat. The sound of her heartbeat. The sound of Viv saying, "I'll call you back."

I didn't hear the patio door open.

I stop kissing Faith and turn to Viv.

Both women have their attention on me. Four beautiful eyes staring at me, all with a yearning and a burning hellfire if I don't say the right thing.

I am master of my fate perhaps, but I'm a horrible captain when it comes to my destiny. I look at both, trying to find the correct response somewhere inside of them.

"I said what I said. I don't take any of it back," whispers Faith.

Viv looks at Faith, trying to read her said words while stabbing her with her eyes. Trying to piece together what was said between us. Trying to find the words to say that will sway me.

But why are two women vying for my affection, wanting me to be with them?

Viv is new and incredible, and our slate is still without a gash, unchipped. She cares for me as I care for her.

Faith has always been that one. The one. *The* one. The one that got away. Can that one become someone new? Can a man have more than one lost love?

I respond the only way I know how. I stand up. I look at them both for a moment, searching their eyes and their souls for the answer to my life's dilemma.

"I have to go" is all I say.

I grab the bag Faith returned and walk off. The women stand there and stare in silent dumbfounded-ness at the audacity of my actions. I get into my car and drive off.

I pull out onto Route 192 and turn right. I watch in my rearview mirror as two wonderful women remain motionless, uncertain of what just happened. Unsure of why I was able to leave them with no answers.

Viv had driven through a hurricane to save me from myself. She's overlooked my past, which seems like that should be automatic. But I find that most people, while they say they are okay with someone's history and they tout live and let live and shit, in reality, their inner judgmental self wins. But Viv, she ultimately seemed okay with it. Because as she puts it, I "came from a time when things like that were cool."

That's the thing about her that has me so intrigued: her ability to separate me from my sins, to see the person I am in spite of all my past mistakes, or despite all my past mistakes. But I am not sure this is one of those mistakes she'll be able to look past. Maybe they will both show up at the party tonight and let bygones be bygones. But that's not likely. Perhaps I screwed the pooch on this one. Though, I was just trying to have a drink by myself before joining the evening's festivity set-up and final preparations. Now I wonder if the fading view from my rearview mirror will be the last time I see either of them.

As Faith and Viv fade from sight, I turn my sights back to the road and traffic. Something in my mind emerges, making me think of the storm. Of Viv and her roommate. Of that thought that escaped my mind. This city of Orlando. The perfect placement of it in the state of Florida. Dead center, as if demanding attention from everything else that is great about the state. I start thinking of the parks, the castle, the rodent, the dynasty, and the man who built the brand. I described it as a machine of beautiful hate. I said that because of the outward beauty it portrays, projects. It fights every second of every day to have every living, breathing member of this world see it as that beautiful creature it wants to be and not as the hateful, mechanized system it can be. The racism thinly veiled in old crow characters, the womanizing and misogyny of the man himself drawn out as a character with a cleft chin. The health-jeopardizing heat the employees must work in day in and day out. The vast amounts of land and ecosystems they destroyed to build their empire on.

And I think of this organism that defines Orlando, and I think of myself. Throughout the years I've cultivated this image, this persona of someone, like anyone in the entertainment industry, you find your crowd and appeal to them. The mass appeal. The journey of getting there, though. That's what makes me think of myself while pondering this place. The pain that I've caused. The months and years lost to alcohol-induced anger, the fights, the bruises, broken bones, the blood, sweat, and tears. All of it to make something that is, in the end, bigger than myself. Greater than any one person. But the hate, the pain that I had to produce to create such beauty, I was the machine. Unintentionally, I was producing the hate that kept the image of me so beautiful. The public image that has people come up to me on the street and give me their praise. It is a realization too many years too late. But I think on this: *Am I starting a cycle over? Is Viv going to stay and be a new Faith? Is there, perhaps, more to this story than cyclical self-destruction?* All I know is that without the chaos of it all, my work would not be what it is. I can't regret that, and I stand by those decisions. Maybe too much. But I do.

I think in each of us there is that beautiful person who causes so much pain without wanting to. Most of the time without realizing it, but we do. And when we finally face the hate we made some people feel, the pain we caused others, only then can we begin to break the cycle that keeps us moving in the same direction.

As I pull up to the valet at the grand event for the evening and toss him my keys, I realize I may have driven around longer than I thought. They are setting up the zones for valet and drop-off. The posters already line the walls and windows. Merchandise booths set up right inside. I exit my car and head through the doors. D.B. and his band have taken up post not far from the exit, talking to my contact.

She tells me that everything is set. I hand her the check that has been in my back pocket. She smiles and assures me that this will be a success.

That everything is going to be fine.

I can only hope.

Finn will return in the second book,
The Fortunate Finn Fairlane

The Fairlane Series:
The Fortunate Finn Fairlane
The Fragile Finn Fairlane

The West Haven Undead Series
Us Of Legendary Gods
So We Stay Hidden
The West Haven Undead.

A Comedy, Noir-style Reverse Harem titled
World Whore, D.

About the Author

Nick Savage lives in the Orlando area with his wife and two cats. He is an award-winning and best-selling author who writes both modern romance and contemporary fantasy. He is also an artist and video game nerd. Follow on Facebook @ SavageWritings, Instagram @TheAuthorNickSavage, and Twitter @SavageWrites.

BOOK CLUB QUESTIONS

1. Which characters in the book did you like best?

2. Which characters did you like least?

3. If you were making a movie of this book, who would you cast as Finn and Faith?

4. With all the music references throughout this book, do you think you'll look up any you aren't familiar with? If so, any in particular?

5. What do you think of the book's cover? How well does it convey what the book is about? If you have seen the previous covers, which one do you like best?

6. Did you find the ending of the book satisfying?

7. How does the setting contribute to the story?

8. Did you guess the ending of the book, and if so, how?

9. What do you think happens to the characters after the book ends?

10. Which parts of the book stood out to you?